S0-AZC-263

KITTY CONFIDENTIAL

Pet Whisperer P.I.

MOLLY FITZ

© 2019, MOLLY FITZ.

All rights reserved. Except as permitted under the U.S. Copyright Act of 1976, no part of this publication may be reproduced, distributed or transmitted in any form or by any means, or stored in a database or retrieval system without the prior written permission of the publisher.

Editor: Megan Harris
Cover Designer: Lou Harper, Cover Affairs
Proofreader: Jasmine Jordan

This is a work of fiction. Names, characters, organizations, places, events, and incidents are either products of the author's imagination or are used fictitiously. Any resemblance to actual persons, living or dead, or actual events is purely coincidental.

No part of this work may be reproduced, or stored in a retrieval system, or transmitted in any form or by any means, electronic, mechanical, photocopying, recording, or otherwise, without written permission of the publisher.

SWEET PROMISE PRESS
PO BOX 72
BRIGHTON, MI 48116

AUTHOR'S NOTE

Hey, new reader friend!

Welcome to the crazy inner workings of my brain. I hope you'll find it a fun and exciting place to be.

If you love animals as much as I do, then I'm pretty sure you're going to enjoy the journey ahead.

Kitty Confidential is just the first of many brain-tickling adventures to come, so make sure you sign up for my newsletter or download my app to help you stay in the know. Doing so also unlocks adorable pictures of my own personal feline over-lord, Schrödinger, deleted scenes from my books, bonus giveaways, and other cool things that are just for my inner circle of readers.

You can download my free app here:
mollymysteries.com/app

Or sign up for my newsletter here:
mollymysteries.com/subscribe

Okay, ready to talk to some animals and solve some mysteries?

Let's do this!
Molly Fitz

To anyone who wishes she could talk to her animal best friend... Well, what's stopping you?

CHAPTER ONE

The first thing you should know about me is that I hate lawyers. The second is that I work for them.

I didn't plan it that way. Not one bit.

I was going to be a huge star, leave Blueberry Bay behind without so much as a farewell glance over my shoulder as I booked it the heck out of there. The problem with that plan was, well, you need talent in order to be a star—and I never had much of that. At least not that I've discovered.

Yet.

When the temp agency assigned me to work for Fulton, Thompson, and Associates as their new paralegal, I almost said no. But then I saw those dollar signs and remembered how rent is a thing that exists.

And so here I am, doing the needful to get by as I continue down that elusive path toward fame by eliminating every possible talent one at a time. Stands to reason, if I keep at it long enough, I'll eventually find my true calling. Who knows? I could be the world's best hip-hop yodeler...

Except I already tried that and I'm not.

It's fine, really. I'm enjoying the journey, although I sure do wish the destination would hurry up and get here already.

Hi, I'm Angie Russo, and one day you're going to see my name in lights.

You see, my nan used to be a celebrated Broadway actress back in the day. That is, until she quit at the peak of her career to retire to Glendale, Maine, and raise her family.

Before you ask, no, I can't sing, dance, or act, but Nan assures me that I have star power in my blood. Just like she did and just like my mom.

Oh, yeah, you probably know my mom. She's the news anchor on Channel Seven and my dad does the sports report. Seeing as they're these huge career types, it was Nan who did most of the work raising me—and that suited me just fine.

In fact, I'd still be living with her even now if she hadn't given me a gentle push out of the nest and told me it was time to fly.

That was about a year ago and happened just shortly after I collected my seventh consecutive associate degree from Blueberry Bay Community College. Yes, indeed, I've always loved learning anything I could wrap my brain around.

At least God did me a solid by making me smart, even if He made my unique talents hard to find. One of my degrees is, in fact, for paralegal studies and law administration services, which may seem like a strange thing to study for someone who hates lawyers as much as I do.

But that's a story for another time…

This is the story of how I almost died, and it's a good one.

I began my day by sniff-testing two blazers with the goal of choosing whichever was cleanest for a will reading at the office that day. Both smelled vaguely of sweat and gym shoes, meaning either would earn me a stern lecture from the partners. Then again, maybe that's precisely what I deserved for putting off that trip to the dry cleaner's for so long.

After spraying a cough-inducing fog of deodorizer into my closet, I plucked the neon pink jacket off its hanger and pushed my arms into the sleeves. A black and white polka dot blouse and stretchy leggings completed the outfit perfectly. Because I didn't have time to wash my hair that morning, I pulled my poofy shoulder-length hair into a messy bun and accented the do with a cute barrette I picked up earlier in the week from my favorite dollar store.

And before you can ask...

No, I didn't have time for dry cleaning.

And, yes, I always had time for the dollar store.

On that particular morning, I didn't have time for either one, though. In fact, I'd spent so much time agonizing over which blazer to wear that I'd pretty much run out of time altogether. I'm already not a morning person, but when you add in a manic rush to get to a job I don't even like...

Well, I could already tell just how bad this day would end up.

I raced out the door—unshowered, unfed, and uncaffeinated—hoping that I'd at least have some luck and catch all green lights on my commute that day. Instead, the longest train in the world cut me off not even two blocks from my house. The train tracks run along the only major street to serve our small coastal town, and there's absolutely no way for me to reach the firm via backroads, which meant I found myself stuck waiting in a line of angry, honking cars for a solid fifteen minutes.

By the time I actually reached the office, I was the last one through the door and we had less than ten minutes until the will reading commenced. My hope to sneak in undetected proved unfounded as well.

"Russo!" Mr. Thompson bellowed before the door even closed all the way behind me. If you pictured an old, white guy wearing boat shoes and an ascot, you'd have a pretty good idea of how Mr. Thompson looked and an even better idea of how he acted. He was a fantastic lawyer, but not a very personable boss.

A thick, meaty vein pulsed at the side of his head, and for some reason I couldn't stop staring at it. He pointed at me with a shaking finger and a scowl. "Late and dressed like you're attending an 80's themed party instead of a will reading. Nope. That's not going to fly today. Go see if Peters has a jacket you can borrow."

It took the strength of a thousand body builders not to roll my eyes as I slumped off to find the only female associate in the whole place.

We often got grouped together by nature of our shared gender, but Bethany Peters and I were nothing alike. She was blonde and pretty and *looked* like she should be sweet as pie, too—except she was actually the biggest shark of them all. I guess you have to be in order to get taken seriously in a man's world.

But what did I know?

I was just a glorified secretary who didn't even want to be there.

Bethany turned her nose up at me the second I entered her office, and I pinched my fingers over mine. See, Bethany had an obsession with essential oils and even sold them in these tacky online parties that she invited us all to about once per month. Even at that point I'd only worked at the firm for a few months but had already ordered more lavender bath salts than I could ever possibly need.

On the day of the will reading, Bethany's office reeked of juniper and lemon—definitely not one of her better combinations. Still, whatever blend of restorative girl power mojo she was trying to concoct, I sincerely hoped it would work for her.

"Let me guess," she said in that nasally, condescending tone that she always used whenever talking to me or one of the other employees without a law degree. "Fulton sent you in to borrow a jacket from me."

A smile crept across my face. "Thompson, actually." Call me a contrarian, but I loved getting the chance to prove her wrong, especially when a day started off as bad as this one had. It was a small and beautiful gift.

"Can't you pick up some more appropriate work clothes for yourself so you're not always stuck borrowing mine last minute?" She sighed before lumbering over to the other side of her office with loose arms and large, exaggerated strides. She looked like a preppy blonde gorilla, but I decided to keep that particular comparison to myself.

"Thompson... Fulton... They're both kind of freaking out today," Bethany confided in me. "Apparently the old lady that died is related to Fulton."

"How do you know?" My eyes grew wide. So, this was why everyone was making such an unusually large fuss that morning.

"Well for starters, her last name is Fulton, too."

She tapped on her temple to draw my attention to her superior brain power.

I tapped on my head and shot her an ugly grimace in response. Now we were both office gorillas, and what an exhibit the pair of us made.

Bethany chuckled as she handed me the most boring navy-blue blazer God ever put on this green earth. "Try to keep it together for the reading, huh?"

I nodded while switching jackets. The blazer pinched at my armpits, but I knew better than to complain. "Thanks," I muttered, narrowly escaping Bethany's office before she could once again remind me that Goodwill or the Salvation Army were nice places to find clothes within my budget.

"I'd lose the barrette!" she shouted after me.

Aargh, so close.

But since Bethany tended to be like a dog with a bone once she had an idea, I pulled my cute little accessory out, taking a few caught hairs with it. The bun came out next, and I quickly finger combed my hair to make it semi-presentable. Hopefully that would be enough to make everyone happy.

"Angie, is that you?" Mr. Fulton, the senior most partner called from inside the conference room. For whatever reason, Thompson always uses our last names, and Fulton sticks to our firsts. Maybe that was their way of playing good lawyer, bad lawyer, or maybe they just liked to keep us on our toes.

I put on my best smile. After all, the guy did just lose a family member. "Good morning, sir. Can I help you with something?"

His eyes lingered on my face briefly before he cleared his throat and pointed to the dusty old coffeemaker in the corner of the room. "We're going to need lots of coffee, and since you're a bit late this morning, I'm afraid there's no time to make a run to the barista. You'll have to use our backup maker. As strong as you can make it, please."

"I'm on it!" We didn't use the in-house coffeemaker very often and really only kept it around for code red caffeine emergencies. The fact we needed it now was definitely not a good sign.

In fact, I'd never actually used that old thing at all. The one time I'd almost had the chance, an intern burst into the office carrying a tray of Star-bucks and let me off the hook. This ancient thing shouldn't be too hard to figure out, though. After all, I had seven associate degrees.

Mr. Thompson, Bethany, and a few of the other associates entered while I was fiddling with the roast basket, which for some reason refused to line up with the necessary grooves in the machine. Normally we'd only have one or two attorneys present at a reading, but they seemed to be pulling out all the stops for this one.

Was it just because the person who died was related to one of our partners? Or was something more going on here? My curiosity had definitely been piqued by this point.

Working in my corner, I caught a few snippets of the discussion happening around the conference room table. Our day-to-day conversations at the firm were normally pretty dry, but things sounded refreshingly juicy today.

"Admittedly, it is a somewhat unusual situation," Thompson said first.

Later, Fulton said, "Given the stipulations, I'm expecting one of the grantees to contest."

An associate named Brad set up a tape recorder —yes, another ancient relic living in our office— and Bethany shuffled a bunch of papers around.

When the coffeemaker's basket snapped into place, I let out a triumphant yip, drawing aggravated stares from my colleagues. "I'll just be right back," I promised as I rushed past the growing crowd with the empty coffee pot.

A beautiful, blonde woman wearing a matching cardigan set and a string of pink pearls stopped me before I could make it to the kitchen tap.

"Angie, I'm so glad I ran into you!" Diane Fulton—Mr. Fulton's wife—shook her head and knitted her over-plucked brow. "Did you catch last night's episode?"

Even though Diane dresses like a blue-blood snob, she was actually the coolest person in the entire place. She and I had a whole list of reality shows we liked to watch together and discuss whenever she came by the office to visit her husband for lunch.

Her eyes widened as she waited for my response. I may have been late to work, but I would never be late when it came to our shows.

"I couldn't believe Trace got eliminated," I answered with a tragic sigh as I turned on the faucet and let water fill the coffeepot. "Hopefully he'll still get a record deal out of the whole thing."

"Let's catch up later," she told me with a slight frown. "I have to..." She pointed to the conference room and knitted her brow again.

And I felt just awful for her. "I heard. My condolences. You, uh, weren't close, were you?"

She stared at me for a moment as if she hadn't

heard the question. Her dangling earrings were so long, they hit her cheeks as she shook her head. "Ethel was Richard's great aunt. She was very old and had been sick for a long time. I think we were all expecting her to go sooner rather than later."

"Still, that sucks," I offered.

Diane gave me a polite smile then excused herself.

Seriously? The best I could come up with was *that sucks?* Good thing none of my degrees were in counseling. Then again, maybe it wouldn't be the worst idea in the world to go back to school. After all, school had always been my happy place. That was part of how I'd ended up with so many degrees to begin with.

I returned with a full carafe of water and a bag of coffee grounds that had expired some time last year but thankfully still smelled fresh. During my very brief absence, the meeting room had filled with even more folks. The Fultons must have been one big family. Either that, or Great Aunt Ethel had been one wealthy--and presumably generous —woman.

Mr. Fulton looked to me with one eyebrow raised in question.

"Almost ready," I assured him as I rushed past

the room of people to my quiet, little coffeemaker corner.

Quick as I could, I filled up the tank with my freshly gotten water, scooped some grounds into the filter, and pressed the big red button to initiate the brewing process.

Nothing happened

So, I pushed it again... and again... and another thirteen times to no effect.

"Plugging it in would help," Bethany shouted loud enough for everyone to hear and causing them all to laugh at me and my well-meaning incompetence.

Ugh, talk about wicked embarrassing!

I groped around the back of the machine until I found the cord. Everyone was still laughing when I pushed the plug into the closest socket...

First, I felt a gentle prick on my fingertips, then my entire body lit with pain. For about two milliseconds, I became hyper-conscious of my surroundings—every smell, sound, feeling, even what the air in that room tasted like just then. The individual laughs transformed into a collective gasp that tore through the room.

Then with a sharp *zzzzztt* it all fell away.

And I fell unconscious to the floor.

CHAPTER TWO

I woke up on the conference room floor. Funny, I couldn't remember passing out, yet there I was.

My heart womped a million miles an hour, but most of my body had become fuzzy and tingly. I tried to move my arms, but they seemed content to lay splayed out at my sides. One by one, my senses started to come back online.

Pop!

Mrs. Fulton's shriek was the first thing I heard, then others in the room began to murmur amongst themselves. Some voices I recognized, but others were completely unfamiliar.

Bethany said, "It's probably time we threw that old thing out."

Mr. Fulton ignored her as he rushed toward me.

"Angie… Angie…" His panicked voice grew closer until he'd arrived right at my side. "Are you okay?"

Meanwhile, Mr. Thompson mumbled something about liabilities and workman's compensation —exactly as anyone who knew him would expect him to do in such a situation.

I was still trying to remember what had happened when an unexpected weight pressed down onto my chest and made it quite difficult for me to breathe. The overpowering smell of tuna filled my nostrils, and the sudden intensity of it brought on a coughing fit.

A voice I'd never heard before hovered over me. "Well, how about that? This one had more than one life, after all. People, *pssh*. So fragile."

"Oh, she's breathing!" Diane shouted.

"Of course, she's breathing, honey," her husband responded with a note of relief in his previously panicked voice. "She's also coughing."

"And here I thought the car trip wouldn't be worth it," that same unfamiliar voice chimed in, pairing the words with an unkind chuckle. "That was, paws down, the best entertainment I've had all week."

Finally, my eyes flew open, and I found a gleaming amber gaze watching me from just a few inches away. Wait... Why was there a cat in the office, and why was it *on me?* I struggled to sit up, but my limbs were still too heavy to lift on my own.

"Oh, honey," that voice drawled again. "If you expect to keep walking, then you probably should have landed on your feet."

I let out a loud groan. I could feel the activity humming all around me, but the only thing I saw was the danged cat who was definitely intruding in my personal space right about then.

"What happened?" I asked before coughing again.

"I think the coffeemaker electrocuted you when you tried to plug it in," Diane revealed. Her shaky voice made it obvious she'd been crying. I felt so bad that my clumsiness put her through that.

"Oh, jeez. This one's even stupider than the first. I'm really looking forward to living with her while the rest of the family figures out where to dump me. Such a pity. They don't know greatness when it's staring them in the face."

I moaned and attempted to lift my head to get a better look around the room. "Who is that?" I demanded.

"It's me, Angie," Mrs. Fulton said, squeezing

one of my hands in earnest. "You asked what happened, and I told you about the coffeemaker."

"No, the guy who just called both of us stupid." I wished I could sit up to see past this annoying cat, but he was the only thing that filled my vision in that moment. Of course, I had lots of questions about the coffeemaker and how such a tiny old appliance had managed to zap me unconscious, but the need to identify the unknown speaker weighed on me much more heavily.

A cruel snicker sounded nearby. "I called you stupid, because you *are* stupid. Honesty is the best policy, the truth will set you free, yada yada, and all that other nonsense you humans like to say."

If I hadn't known any better, I'd have sworn that strange, lilting voice was coming from the cat. Man, how hard had I hit my head when I fell?

The cat leaned in so close that his whiskers tickled my face. His unnervingly large eyes moved frantically from side to side as if stalking some kind of prey. Oh, how I hoped I wasn't that prey. I'd barely escaped the coffeemaker. If something sentient set out to hurt me today, I wouldn't even stand a chance.

"Did you… Did you really hear what I said?" the voice asked again, and again it really sounded like it was coming from the cat. Did he eat a tiny human or something? None of this made any sense.

"Yes, I hear you, and I think you're rather mean," I answered with a huff, giving the best attitude I could, considering my prone position.

"Angie, who are you talking to?" Diane asked with words that sounded unsure and just as worried as I felt myself.

"I'm not sure who it is, but he keeps insulting me." I closed my eyes tight, then slowly opened them again.

The cat seemed to smile, but not in a friendly way. Once again, I wondered if he considered me easy prey. Heck, I considered me easy prey, too.

"No one's insulting you," Mr. Fulton insisted. "We all just want to make sure you're okay."

The cat smiled again, bigger this time. "Ooh, ooh, me! I'm insulting you, you big, stupid bag of skin."

"He just called me a big, stupid bag of skin! Can you really not hear him?" I blinked half a dozen times, then pinched myself. Nothing seemed to change.

"Russo, I think maybe you should take the rest of the day off and a trip to the emergency room,"

Mr. Thompson commanded after clearing his throat loudly from somewhere near the door.

"Wow, you really can hear me," the voice said again. "By the way, hi, I'm Octavius Maxwell Ricardo Edmund Frederick Fulton, and I have some demands."

I was having a difficult time keeping track of all the threads of conversation. I knew the partners were worried about me and about themselves, but I still couldn't identify the mystery speaker or figure out what he wanted. "Octavius Maxwell… who?"

"Honey, are you talking about the cat?" Mrs. Fulton asked, picking the tabby off from my chest.

My straining lungs thanked her, and immediately I felt stronger.

In a cutesy baby voice, Diane held the cat up to her face and cooed, "Are you trying to help our Angie feel better? You're such a sweet fuzzy wuzzy."

The cat turned to me and narrowed his eyes into slits. *"Heeeeelp meeeee."*

Energized at last by my need to find out what the heck was going on, I managed to sit up and look around the room.

"Oh, good. Now that you can move again, Peters will take you to the hospital," Thompson decreed.

Bethany sighed but didn't argue the point.

"Wait!" The tabby cat trotted up to me the second Diane set him back on the floor. "What about my demands?"

I stared at him, dumbfounded. There was absolutely no way...

The cat flicked his tail and emitted a low growl from deep in his throat. "I know you can hear me, so how about doing the polite thing and keeping up your end of the conversation, huh?"

"What do you want?" I whispered, but still everyone in the office could see and hear the crazy lady talking to the cat she'd just met.

"My owner was murdered, and I need you to help me prove it. Also, of equal importance, I haven't been fed in hours. Maybe years." His ears fell back against his head and his eyes widened, making me feel inexplicably fond of him despite his bad attitude.

Then the first part of what he said hit me, and I gasped. *"Murdered?"*

Bethany tittered nervously and grabbed me by the arm. "Okay, let's get you to the hospital. Hallucinations are not a good sign."

"But..." I began to argue. That argument fell

away when I realized I had no sane or valid reason to resist.

"*Murdered!*" the cat shouted after me dramatically. "She was offed before her time, and now that I know you can hear me, you're going to help me get her the justice she deserves. It's the least I can do to thank her for all the years she spent feeding me and arranging my pillows just as I like them. Also, did you hear the part about me needing to be fed?"

Bethany and I had almost made it to the doorway. That meant it was my last chance to talk to the cat. For all I knew, we would never see each other again. Of course, I knew it was totally crazy to assume there was even a chance any of this being real, but still, I couldn't ignore the fact that the talking tabby needed my help.

"I want to help!" I bellowed back into the room just before the door closed behind us.

"No, you *need* help," Bethany growled, sounding even more like an animal than the cat had. "Thanks a lot, by the way. This was the first time they've included me in something this important to the firm. Now, thanks to your little act with the coffeemaker, I'm going to miss it."

That hurt almost as bad as the zap from the

coffeemaker. "You honestly don't think I electrocuted myself just to sabotage you, do you?"

She sighed and pinched the bridge of her nose. "No, I'm sorry. I know it's not your fault. I just have to work twice as hard to get ahead since I'm the only female associate, and everyone wants to put me on the baby track instead of the partner track."

"Yeah, well… at least you're not just some glorified secretary." I honestly couldn't believe Bethany was complaining about *her* problems when I'd just had a near-death experience a few minutes earlier…

Or maybe I could. It was Bethany, after all.

She settled me into the passenger seat of her car. It was a newer model Lexus, which told me she probably didn't have things quite as bad as she thought. Still, I felt guilty for costing her what she considered to be her big shot, so I said, "For what it's worth, you're the smartest one of them all."

She laughed as she buckled her seatbelt and adjusted the rear-view mirror. "Even more than Thompson and Fulton?"

I nodded, and the movement made me dizzy. "Especially more than Thompson and Fulton."

We shared a brief glance of camaraderie before she backed out of her spot and navigated onto the main road. Hopefully there would be no more trains passing through today, because despite our brief bond of sisterhood, I wasn't sure how long either of us could handle being trapped in a car together.

"Thanks for taking me, even though I know you didn't want to. You don't have to wait around. Just drop me off and I'll call my nan to come get me when I'm done."

"Already planned on it. If I hurry, I can still make part of the reading." She tapped at her temple to once again show her superior thinking.

And just like that, we were back to normal.

As for me? I wasn't so sure.

CHAPTER THREE

I sat swinging my legs off the side of a wheeled hospital bed as the emergency room doctor laughed right in my face.

"You actually got electrocuted by an old coffeemaker?" Whatever kind of reception I might have expected to get at the hospital, this definitely wasn't it.

I crossed my arms over my chest and turned away so I wouldn't have to look at his inappropriately amused expression. "Yes, I don't see why that's funny."

He finally sobered up as he twiddled his pen between his fingers like a strange tic. Studying me with a slight frown, he asked, "And it caused you to lose consciousness?"

"Yes." We'd been over this before.

"Did you hit your head on the way down?"

"I don't think so." There was still plenty about my accident I couldn't quite wrap my head around, but at least I felt fine physically.

The doctor stuck his pen back into his pocket and peered into my eyes before declaring, "Well, you look okay to me. The most I'd prescribe to you is a dose of regular strength Tylenol in case there's any pain from hitting the floor like you did."

He hesitated for a moment, then shook his head and offered a wry laugh. "It's strange, though… the voltage in that coffeemaker should have only given you a light zap. I'm surprised you had such a strong reaction."

So, we were back to this. I needed to get out of there before he called in his entire staff to check out the freak on display in the ER.

"Gee, thanks," I muttered.

His vision narrowed. "Yes, *thanks* is right. Be thankful you haven't got any burns. No concussion, either. But you did manage to score a day off work, huh?" The doctor had the audacity to wink at me before letting out another chuckle and turning to walk away.

"I didn't do this to myself on purpose!" I called

after him, trying not to let my frustration get the better of me. *What a jerk.*

When I was sure he wouldn't be coming back, I shot a quick text to Nan and gathered my things to go wait for her outside. The whole time I sat there waiting, I didn't see a single person come or go through those spinny glass doors. Even though Blueberry Bay wasn't the most densely populated area, I still expected the hospital to see some activity. Then again, maybe it was a good thing that clown of a doctor didn't have any actual sick people to look after.

I paced back and forth along the curb, trying my best to recall every detail of that morning. As unkind as the doctor had been, he did have a point. I'd nearly died at the hands of an old coffeemaker, and when I'd woken up again, I could talk to animals.

As a kid, I'd loved watching Eddie Murphy as the hapless Dr. Doolittle, helping his animal patients like no one else could thanks to his unique ability to talk with them. Back then, I'd thought it would be so cool to be able to understand and hold conversations with animals.

But now that I was faced with the reality?

I was scared out of my mind.

A strong gust of wind kicked up a swirl of leaves, drawing my attention to the parking lot where a pair of seagulls fought beak and talon over a fast-food hamburger wrapper that appeared to have a bit of cheese stuck to its center.

One of them held its wings out to his side and screeched. Then the other hissed and pecked at his opponent's feet. Their fight took on new vigor as they danced around the wrapper screaming and pecking at each other—and giving me the beginnings of a wicked headache.

"Oh, will you just be quiet!" I shouted at them.

If the birds could hear me, they were clearly too occupied with their impromptu battle to care.

Wait… could they hear me? Would they be able to talk to me like the cat from work did?

I tiptoed over to them, thankful I was on my own in the abandoned parking lot because I knew how crazy I looked in that moment. Still, a little crazy was a small price to pay for finally figuring out what was going on with me today.

I cleared my throat and addressed the birds. "Excuse me."

One of the seagulls cawed and nipped at the other, but neither of them gave me any credence.

"Excuse me," I called a little louder, taking several more steps forward.

One of the birds turned to look at me, and the other took the opportunity to grab the wrapper and hop away with it. The first gave chase and soon the two were locked in a tug of war, the paper wrapper twisting and crinkling between them.

I chased after them too and yelled at the top of my lungs, *"Excuse me!"*

Finally, they both gave me their attention, although neither let go of the coveted prize.

Since I at last knew they were listening, I followed up with an offer I knew they wouldn't be able to refuse. I smiled wide and told them, "I have tons of tasty food. Burgers, fries, ice cream cones... It's all yours if you just answer one question: *Can you understand me?"*

One of the gulls tilted its head as if to think about this. While he was distracted, the other yanked the wrapper free and flew off into the sky.

"Sorry about that," I told the remaining bird. "I can get you more food, better food that didn't come from the trash. What do you say?"

Before the gull could answer, a ruby red sports coupe rolled up next to me, scaring him off once and for all.

Nan rolled down the window of her favorite new toy and whistled at me. "Hop in, dearie!"

"Thanks for coming to get me." I slid onto the slippery leather seat and tugged the seatbelt across my chest.

Nan let the car idle as she lowered her cat eye sunglasses and studied me without saying a word. Her blue-gray hair was covered with a brightly patterned silk scarf, and she wore driving gloves that matched the exact same shade of red as the car's exterior. I had to admit, Nan had style. Even when she'd moved away from the spotlight of Broadway, she'd never stopped putting on a show.

I shrugged. "What? I'm fine."

Additional wrinkles formed on her forehead. "You didn't say much in your text. What happened?"

"Just a mild electric shock. Again, I'm fine."

She raised an eyebrow at me. "Then why the hospital?"

I shrugged again. "You know how the partners are. They don't want to take any risks when it comes to liabilities and whatnot."

She shook her head, then stepped on the gas pedal so hard it jerked us both back against our seats. "So where to?"

I needed to find that cat since it seemed only he had the answers I craved. If I was lucky, then this would all turn out to be one very bad dream. Either way though, I had to know—but Nan didn't. At least not until I knew how to explain what was happening to me.

"Back to the office, please," I answered, fingering my seatbelt nervously.

Nan let out a sassy little huff. "C'mon, not even going to take the full day off? You've already been excused, now let's play hooky. Maybe we could hit the beach. Or perhaps a matinee. What do you say, dear?"

Ah, playing hooky. That had always been Nan's favorite thing. Some of my favorite childhood memories involved her breaking me out of second period to go on some zany, ill-conceived adventure. As I'd grown older, our skip days had grown fewer and far between. In fact, we hadn't managed a single one since I'd moved out to get my own place.

Make no mistake, I missed my nan dearly. However…

I hated to let her down, but I had no other choice. "That sounds great, but I've got to grab my car from the office or I'll have a hard time of it tomorrow. Maybe I could meet you for dinner instead?" I offered with the biggest smile I can muster.

Nan groaned and took a sharp right turn. "This new job has changed you."

Oh, she had no idea.

Despite Nan's objections, she brought me back to the office in one piece. Hardly more than an hour had passed since I left and most everyone was still hanging around, discussing the surprise twists in Ethel Fulton's will. Could one of them really be a murderer?

Only my new cat friend had the answers, which is why it was so important that I find him without any further delays or interruptions.

I spotted Bethany chatting with the other associates and headed her way to ask that they fill me in on what I missed.

"Can you believe she left so much to the cat? What's a cat going to do with all that money?" someone I didn't recognize grumbled, taking a long pull at his take-out coffee cup.

The woman standing beside him nodded. "It's a real slap in the face."

Who are these two? Could they be the murderers? I wondered, trying not to stare as I committed their features to memory.

Diane came out of nowhere and saddled me with a giant, squishy hug. "Oh, thank goodness you're okay. We were all so worried!"

"Yup, you'll need more than an angry coffeemaker to take me out. I'm made of tougher stuff." I knocked on my collarbone to demonstrate my durability.

As much as I enjoyed my chats with Diane, I came back for one reason and one reason alone—to find that cat. Somehow, I had to figure out a way to inquire about him without raising anyone's suspicions.

"Um, did the reading go okay?" I fished, hoping she would take the bait and swim with it.

Mrs. Fulton dropped her voice to a whisper and leaned in close. "Yes, but some of the relatives are upset with their take. You know how these things are."

"At least she didn't leave it all to the cat." I tried to act casual, seeing as I'd already overheard that the dearly deceased had done exactly that.

"Well, not all of it, but it was still quite a bit. That's why he was here, you know. She required all beneficiaries be present and seeing as the cat was one of the biggest, well, there you go."

I feigned shock—not the electrocution kind this time, but the real, honest-to-goodness surprise at receiving unexpected news. "You've got to be kidding me."

Diane shook her head and made a funny face. "Never let it be said that Auntie Fulton didn't love that cat."

"So, what's going to happen to him now that she's gone?"

Mr. Fulton noticed us and crossed the office to join our conversation. "Back already, Angie? Don't you at least want to take the rest of the day off?"

Crud. I'd been so close to getting the answer I needed from his wife. Now I had to find a way to steer the discussion back to the location of that cat without making things too awkward. Mr. Fulton was a smart guy who regularly bested the area's top attorneys in court. Did I really think I could outmaneuver him?

I had to try.

I swallowed hard and put on the same semi-famous smile that had landed me this job in the first place. "I'm fine. I'll probably head out early but wanted to check in first to grab my car and let you all know I'm okay."

"Great. See you tomorrow, then. Sleep in a little if you think it will help." Mr. Fulton patted me on the shoulder and glanced pointedly toward the door.

I knew he was just looking out for me, but I couldn't leave without first talking to that cat, especially if there was a murderer afoot. Hopefully Mr. Fulton would thank me for my stubbornness on this matter later.

I stood my ground, twisting my hands before me. "Actually, I was wondering if the cat was still around. He seemed pretty worried, and I wanted to let him know I'm okay."

Husband and wife exchange a worried expression.

"It's okay, dear. We'll tell him for you," Diane informed me kindly.

I hated lying, but desperate times…

"It may not be okay," I warned then jumped with both feet straight into my lie. "I did a course on Animal Psychology back at Blueberry Bay Community College, and it would help if he could see for himself that I'm fine. Otherwise, um, behavioral problems could arise due to sublimated anxiety."

Mrs. Fulton stared at me in confused horror. "Oh, no, we don't want that!"

Mr. Fulton chuckled. "You said it, honey. Especially since he's staying with us for the foreseeable future. We don't want old Octavius taking out his sublimated anxiety on our new curtains."

And there it was. Another golden opportunity, one I was too greedy not to grab hold of.

"You know... He's probably already quite anxious. More than likely depressed, too, what with his owner dying and his whole life being uprooted."

"I hadn't thought of it like that." Diane's brow pinched with concern. "Can cats get depression?"

I almost had her.

Nodding vigorously, I dug my hooks in deeper. "Most definitely, and since they can't exactly take anti-depressants, they really need someone who knows how to recognize the signs and treat them naturally."

"What are you suggesting?" Mr. Fulton asked. Unfortunately, his face gave nothing away.

Shrugging, I try to act disinterested in the outcome to really sell it now. "I know I'm just a paralegal, but I did take that course and I've always had a way with animals, especially cats. Since you have so much going on with the family and the estate, maybe I should take him off your hands for a few days. I could keep him out of your hair and help him work through his depression, if you want."

They looked at each other, exchanging a look I couldn't quite discern. I supposed that type of thing came with being married for thirty-plus years.

Diane was the one who finally answered for both of them. "It would be a huge help to us, but are you sure?"

With a massive placating grin, I answered, "It would be my pleasure."

Yes, a pleasure—and hopefully *not* my funeral instead.

CHAPTER FOUR

With the Fultons' blessing, I let myself into the senior partner's office and immediately spotted the cat. He sat right in the center of the leather desk chair like some kind of Bond villain. I half expected him to pull out a smaller, fluffier cat to stroke intimidatingly while he spoke to me.

"Took you long enough," he mumbled, obsessively licking his paw. Despite all I had been through to get back to him, he didn't even bother to look up at me. I'd known this cat for all of five minutes and could already tell that he was a major jerk.

If I'd only been grappling with the talking-to-animals problem that day, I probably would have walked away then and there. But, no, someone had been murdered—and a sweet old lady at that.

"I came as fast as I could," I hissed, wondering how he liked that little dose of his own medicine. "It's not like you had anywhere else to be."

He snorted and said something about busy schedules and important routines. I didn't exactly catch everything because he spoke incredibly fast.

Whatever the case, there I stood, conversing with a cat in a way we both mostly understood. If I was crazy, then at least I was consistent about it. Now that I'd found and confirmed my ability to talk to this cat, it was time to learn his impossibly long moniker. "What's your name again?"

He rolled his amber eyes then rose to his feet. "Weren't you paying attention? I'm Octavius Maxwell Ricardo Edmund Frederick Fulton."

No wonder he talked so fast. It was the only way for him to spit out that name without risking the other person falling asleep right in the middle of it. I tested out the strange name, hoping that if I got it right he might be a little nicer to me. "Octavius Maxwell Richard…"

"Ricardo Edmund Frederick Fulton," he corrected. "Honestly, it's not that hard."

He hopped off the chair and paced toward me,

irritation flashing in his snake-like eyes. Somehow it was now my fault he had a ridiculous long name. Well, I refused to be bullied by a creature that I easily outweighed ten-to-one.

"My name's Angie. Thanks for asking, by the way."

He stopped walking and crinkled the skin above his nose. "Well, that's boring. It's got no ring to it at all."

"Sorry to disappoint you," I hissed, which made me wonder if I was speaking cat or if he was speaking human.

The tabby's voice took on a kinder tone for the first time since I'd met him. He sighed, and said, "Well, we can't all be Octavius Maxwell Ricardo Edmund Frederick Fulton, the First."

"Wait, did you just add to your name to make it longer? No, this is not going to work. Even if I could remember your string of, like, eight names, I am not saying all of them whenever I want to get your attention."

"Whatever." He widened his eyes at me and yawned. What a bratty cat. Hopefully, if I put him in his place, he'd start treating me as an equal instead of an incompetent servant.

"Since you're on board, I'm shortening your

name to… to… *umm…*"

"Nice to see your mind is just as sharp as your name." He let out a mewling laugh, which I ignored.

"Shut up, Octavius… Octagon… Octopuss… Octo-Cat! That's it. From now on, I'll call you Octo-Cat." I felt so proud of myself for that cute nickname that fit him like a glove. Not even his bad attitude could bring me down now.

"Octo… Cat." He sneered and batted at the air between us. "I don't think so."

"Well, your first name is Octavius, and you have like eight names total, so—"

He padded the ground and spun in a circle. "No, my first name is Octavius Maxwell Ric—"

"*Enough!* Do you want me to go back to Octo-Puss? Because I can."

He began to say something, but the sound of the door creaking open stopped us both mid-conversation.

Diane's head appeared in the doorway before the rest of her. "Everything okay in here? I thought I heard voices."

I stood up straight and brushed off the knees of my pants, flashing my friend with an ingratiating smile to promise I wasn't crazy. "Totally fine. I was just introducing myself and letting him know he's going to be living with me for a few days."

She glanced toward Octo-Cat, who chose that exact moment to plop himself on his rump and start licking his kitty bits. "You're talking to the cat?" she asked, but it didn't really sound like a question.

I fixed my eyes on her to show I wasn't embarrassed, even though I mostly definitely was. "Of course. It helps them to forge an emotional bond which will be important even for the brief time we're living together."

She glanced from me to the cat and back again, then shrugged. "Okay, well, I just pulled his things from the car. Are you sure it's not any trouble for you to take him off our hands for a few days?"

She stopped and frowned before confiding, "I'm afraid he's not the nicest animal."

"*Positive.* Thanks for grabbing his stuff. I should probably get both of us home for some rest. Busy day, huh?" I laughed nervously, then pushed past her through the doorway.

"Here, kitty. C'mon, kitty." I clicked my tongue and patted the side of my thigh to call him over.

Octo-Cat obediently trotted after me, mumbling through gritted teeth, "If you ever call me 'kitty' again, I'm going to puke in your slippers while you sleep."

"Okay, bye now!" I yelled to Diane, quickly gathering up all of the cat's things piled by the firm's main entrance.

Once we were both safely seated in my car, Octo-Cat exploded in a litany of what I assumed were feline-specific curse words.

"Stop that," I scolded. "Didn't your mother teach you any manners?"

He paused and looked over at me with such derision, I actually recoiled. "Now you're insulting my mother? I'll have you know she did the best she could with seven kittens to feed and only six nipples to feed them with."

I shuddered and pulled the car into reverse. "Well, thank you for that visual."

Octo-Cat let out a terrible yowl and jumped onto my lap, claws extended. "Oh, my whiskers! We're going to die!" he cried. "I'm too young to die. Too pretty. And far too important."

"Aww, are you afraid?" I cooed, almost liking him in that moment, even though his claws were digging into my thigh. "That's so cute."

"I am not cute," he ground out. "Get me to

safety at once, then we shall discuss your punishment."

I laughed and turned on the radio, letting the newest top forty hit flood the car and drown out some of Octo-Cat's complaints about my driving.

Despite the unnecessary drama, we managed to make it back to my house in good time, but now I had a new problem. I loved my tiny two-bedroom rental with its wide porch and tall oak tree in the front yard.

My new roommate, on the other hand...

"Where have you brought me?" he demanded, unwilling to leave the car no matter how much I begged.

"This is my house and you'll be living here, too, for a few days," I explained, even though my patience had worn so thin it was like a strand of angel hair pasta.

He turned his spoiled pink nose up at me. "No, absolutely not! This is hardly even a hovel. It's not up to the standards by which I am accustomed to living."

I had half a mind to hightail it back to the office and return him to the Fultons. Instead I took a deep, sarcastic bow and grumbled, "Well, too bad, your royal highness. This is all I can afford. Besides, you're just an ordinary tabby cat with a bad attitude and ridiculous expectations of life."

He hissed and took an honest-to-goodness swipe at me. Luckily, I managed to yank my arm out of his path before he could break skin.

"Just a tabby!" he shouted, gracing me with another diatribe full of kitty curses. "How dare you? I'll have you know that I am part Maine Coon on my grandmother's side."

I was growing really tired of this. Why did every little thing have to be a battle?

I dropped to my haunches to face him eye-to-eye, even though it put me at incredible risk given his temper coupled with those sharp claws.

"Look, do you want me to help you solve this murder or not? Because from where I'm sitting, I'm literally the only person in the entire world who can help you right now. But if you want me to actually do that, you're going to have to be a whole lot nicer."

We stared each other down, but I refused to look away first. I dealt with megalomaniac attorneys on the regular. I could handle this little, ill-tempered cat.

Finally, Octo-Cat stretched, yawned, jumped

down from the car, and trotted over to my front door.

"Are you going to let me in or what?" he yowled from my porch, flicking his tail in agitation.

Well, at least it was progress.

CHAPTER FIVE

Once inside, Octo-Cat made a beeline for my favorite overstuffed armchair. Despite his protests only moments ago, he quickly settled in and made himself comfortable. From the state of my pants, I already knew Octo-Cat was a massive shedder. My poor cream-colored chair didn't stand a chance against his brown and black fur.

Still, he was a guest, and Nan had worked hard to teach me manners.

"Can I get you something to drink?" I asked, hesitating by the kitchen.

He perked his head up and let out a contented purr that I found just as shocking as if he'd sprouted a second tail. "Do you have any Evian?" he asked politely, crossing his paws in front of himself now.

"I have tap water and…" I glanced into the fridge and frowned at the lack of cat-friendly options. "Diet Coke and apple juice, too."

The purring abruptly stopped as Octo-Cat uncrossed and recrossed his paws. "I'll pass for now, but you're going to need to go to the store and gather the necessary supplies for my stay. I only drink Evian, and I only eat Fancy Feast. Not just any flavor, mind you. It must be fish-based, and it must come in the small metal can—not the plastic container. I can taste the difference."

I couldn't help but laugh at the audacity of this request. "Is that all?"

"No, but we need to start somewhere." He scowled at me, refusing to see the humor in the situation.

Seeing as we were getting nowhere fast, I gave up in the kitchen and returned to the living room with a can of Diet Coke for myself. I slumped on the couch with a huge sigh. If Octo-Cat was going to be melodramatic, then I would be, too.

His probing amber gaze bore into me, refusing to look away, and that danged tail began flicking wildly again. It was a wonder he hadn't learned any manners, given the circumstances in which he'd lived up until two days ago.

I cleared my throat but still, he continued to stare unabashedly. Was he waiting for me to…? *Oh my gosh.*

"I don't need to go to the store right now," I snapped, correcting my posture and glaring right back at him. "Do I?"

He shrugged as if he hadn't given it much thought, even though we both knew he had. "Well, it would be nice."

"This morning all you could talk about was Ethel Fulton's murder. Now it's more important that you have a specific type of water than that we discuss the details and start working on the case?"

He considered this for a moment. "I never thought I'd say this, but bring on the tap water."

"Really?" Despite his giving the desired response, I fully expected him to change his mind within a matter of seconds—or to tell me that he'd obviously been joking and then call me stupid for not getting it.

"Sometimes we have to make sacrifices for the ones we love. This one's for Ethel." He nodded gravely despite the fact that we were discussing one of the most mundane topics imaginable.

"Oh, how long-suffering you are."

His eyes widened in what I presumed was shock.

"Hopefully not *long* suffering. Once I tell you what I know, it should be an open and shut case."

"Perfect," I said, making my way to the kitchen and running the faucet for a few seconds to make sure it was the perfect temperature for my spoiled new acquaintance. "Tell me what you know."

Octo-Cat waited until I had returned and set the bowl of water on the coffee table before him. He hopped over and sniffed hesitantly.

"This isn't made of Lennox or crystal. Not even stainless steel." He craned his neck to the side, turning his body into an odd, snobby twist of fur and limbs. "What is it? And is it safe to drink from?"

"It's a normal bowl from the dollar store and is perfectly fine. I eat out of it all the time." I pushed the bowl toward him emphatically, and Octo-Cat jumped back in fright.

"That's hardly a ringing endorsement." He eyed me from head to toe and shrugged his little kitty shoulders before turning and leaping back to my armchair. "Suddenly, I'm not so thirsty," he declared with a yawn.

Instead of responding to his snobbery, I popped open my soda and took a nice, long drink. The bubbles did little to calm my frazzled nerves.

"Are we going to talk about this?" Octo-Cat flicked his tail impatiently. Despite the many delays he'd caused, my single drink was now to blame for us falling behind in the two of us beginning our job as amateur sleuths.

As much as I hated to be a pushover, it was simply easier to go along with his outrageousness than to keep arguing over every little thing. The sooner we identified the murderer and brought him to justice, the sooner I could be back to my normal, cat-free life.

I took a deep, centering breath and asked, "What makes you think Ethel Fulton was murdered?"

"I don't *think* she was murdered. I *know* it. I saw everything with my own two eyes." He widened his amber gaze demonstratively. Maybe this wouldn't be so difficult after all.

"Oh, great. Well, who did it then?" I leaned forward, ready for the big reveal.

"I don't know."

Deep breaths. "But you said you saw everything?"

"I did."

"Then how can you not know who did it?"

"It was definitely a human," he said, an expression of surety spread between his whiskers.

"Really? Is that all you've got?" The couch groaned in protest as I threw myself back against it and threw my hands in the air so as not to ring Octo-Cat's neck with them. "Was it a man or a woman? Someone old or young? A stranger or someone she knew?"

He yawned. "Do you really expect me to remember that?"

"Are you serious?" And now I was yelling at a cat.

"What? It's not my fault all humans look the same."

Deep, calming yoga breaths. "So, you saw a human kill her, but you don't know who."

"Yes. That's what I said. Aren't you paying attention?"

I spoke slowly even though he was the one who assumed me to be an idiot. "Do you know how the human killed her? From what I understand, she died of natural causes."

"No, she wasn't ready to die yet. Someone definitely intervened."

I waited for him to say more, but he started grooming himself instead.

"Hello? We're kind of in the middle of an important conversation here. Can you stop licking yourself for five minutes so we can figure this out?"

Octo-Cat let out a little huff but complied with my request. "The sacrifices I make. I hope Ethel is watching from above so that my good deeds don't go unnoticed."

"I'm sure she's in Heaven, looking down at us and thinking, 'Wow, what a great cat I had.' Now, can you tell me the whole story from start to finish? *About the murder,*" I quickly specified, not wanting to hear about his mother's six nipples again.

He nodded and brought himself up onto his haunches. What followed was a dramatic retelling that would have been worthy of an Oscar if anyone could understand him besides me.

"Let me paint the scene for you." He lifted his paw and swept it in an arc before him. "It was just two nights ago. The weather was balmy. The light had begun to fade from the sky. Ethel had invited several other humans over to eat food at the table. She cooked the whole thing herself. I remember because she made salmon and also gave me a little plate to enjoy. I'm happy to report the fish was perfectly cooked, tender but not dry, and the portion was absolutely perfect, too. Ethel always knew exactly what I needed."

"Focus, please," I said through gritted teeth. "Back to the murder, if you don't mind."

He sneered but didn't offer any verbal argument. "Everyone ate more than their fill, then they all went home. When Ethel was getting ready for bed, she clutched her chest and told me she wasn't feeling well, then tucked herself in and went to sleep. She didn't wake up again."

"It sounds like maybe she had a heart attack. What makes you think she was murdered?" I reached out to offer him a conciliatory pat on the head, but he batted my hand away.

"Ethel had a very strong heart," he insisted. "She was always telling me about it after she came back from the doctors." He made his voice high and scratchy, hunching forward in what seemed to be an impression of his late owner. "'Doc says I have a strong heart and just might live forever.' In fact, she went to the doctor just that week, and he again told her what good shape her heart was in."

I didn't know how to put this delicately, so I just blurted it out. "Yes, but she was old. Sometimes their bodies just give out on them."

He shook his head adamantly, and when he glanced up at me again, his eyes had crossed before his nose. "Maybe, but that's not what happened to Ethel. She smelled funny after dinner."

I worried my lip while thinking this over. I knew Octo-Cat loved his owner, but the more he talked, the more it sounded as if she'd died of natural causes and not some secret murder scheme. I just didn't know how to tell him this.

After a moment's hesitation, I told him, "I've heard cats can sometimes know when people are about to die. You two were very close, so maybe you just sensed it."

Again with the manic head shaking. "No, she was definitely murdered. That same weird smell was in the dinner and the tea."

"Are you trying to tell me she was poisoned? I'm not sure that pans out. Remember, you told me in great detail how you ate the fish and you are perfectly fine."

"She fed me before the guests arrived. I think someone tampered with the food after I'd left the kitchen to go take a catnap."

I raised an eyebrow and asked, "Then why didn't the other guests die?"

"Someone specifically wanted to kill Ethel, I guess." He moved his eyes to the chair before him in his first show of true sorrow. "I don't understand.

She was the nicest human ever. Who would want to kill her?"

"I was hoping you'd know the answer to that one." I had to remind myself that he didn't want to be petted—at least not by me. I wrapped both hands around my drink and took another sip before suggesting, "She did have a lot of money. Do you think someone was trying to get their inheritance early?"

His head whipped back up and his eyes focused in on mine. "So, you think someone in the family killed her?"

I shrugged. "I'm still not entirely convinced she was even murdered."

"Then I guess I'm going to have to show you." He popped to his feet and jumped off the chair in what amounted to the blink of an eye.

"Show me? How?" I asked, following dumbly.

"Let's go to my house and take a look around. I guarantee you'll find the proof you need," he said, then flicked his tail before adding, "Seeing as my word apparently isn't enough."

CHAPTER SIX

I considered it a small miracle that Octo-Cat actually knew his home address. He and Ethel had lived together on the exact opposite side of town close to the bay—the same as all the other wealthy folks around Glendale.

A private drive twisted about half a mile through the woods before it opened up to a gorgeous, sprawling Colonial with huge bay windows looking out onto the sea.

My jaw dropped in response to the unexpected grandeur. "You live here?"

"Safety first, then talk," Octo-Cat whisper-yelled, digging his claws deeper into my thighs as I navigated the last stretch of driveway and pulled to a stop before the structure that reminded me more of a palace than an actual home.

Rather than parking out front, I pulled around to the far side of the house to at least partially conceal my visit. As soon as I opened the car door, Octo-Cat hopped out onto the ground and walked in a crooked line toward the porch.

"Wait!" I called after him, taking another opportunity to survey the estate. "Are we really just going to walk right in?"

"Of course, we are. This is my home."

"Yeah, but isn't it locked?" Despite all my various degrees and random knowledge, I'd never taken the time to learn locksmithing. Perhaps I could add it to my list for later, although that wouldn't help us much now.

"Pssh. Only for humans. Watch." Octo-Cat ran up the porch steps and stood before a little doggie door that was almost perfectly hidden within the stone face of the house. As he waited, the slab slid open, admitting him inside and leaving no doubt that Octo-Cat's front door cost more than my entire month's—maybe even year's—rent.

I jogged up to join him, then lowered myself to my hands and knees to peer inside. The stone doorway shut right in my face but re-opened a few seconds later.

Octo-Cat trotted back outside with a smile curling across his short snout. "It's good to be home."

"Well, don't get used to it. We're only here to look for clues."

"What are you waiting for, then? Come inside." He slipped back in through his private entrance, and this time I was close enough to see a little light flash on his collar before the door slid open. Fancy.

Octo-Cat turned around to glare at me. "Aren't you coming?"

"Just one small problem." I reached my hand in after him. "I don't fit."

He shook his head slowly and raised a paw to his face in exasperation. "Then grab the key that's under the shiny rock. Hurry up already!"

I groaned as I lifted myself back to my feet and searched the porch and nearby flowerbeds for the shiny rock he'd mentioned. Even having only met Octo-Cat earlier that day, I already knew better than to ask for help or further clarification. Honestly, you haven't lived until you've been conde-scended to by a cat—although I don't recommend the experience if you can avoid it.

As for me, I had no choice in the matter. At least not until I either solved the murder or proved no foul play had occurred, either of which I considered an equally likely outcome.

Octo-Cat jogged back out and tapped my calf with his paw. He made no effort to conceal his claws when doing so. "You're looking in the wrong place," he informed me with a bored expression.

I glared down at him and checked my leg for any fresh pricks of blood.

My kitty companion spun in a circle then hopped off the porch and began pawing at the corner where the house met the steps. There sat the first in a series of foot path lights, none of which had been illuminated despite the descending dusk.

I trotted back down the steps after him and pulled that first light right out of the ground. Sure enough, a small silver key lay buried in the earth beneath. "Good hiding spot," I said as I bent down to pluck the key from its grave.

"Ethel was just as smart as she was kind," Octo-Cat said with a reverence he didn't normally possess. "She really was the best human. Too bad you never got the chance to meet her."

I was just about to tell him how sweet I found

that sentiment, when he added, "You really could have learned so much."

"All right," I said with a grunt, turning to face the stairs once again. "Let's get on with this investigation already."

The key slid into the lock perfectly, and a moment later I stood inside the regal entryway with no clue where to begin. Letting out a low whistle, I whispered, "This place is huge."

Octo-Cat sighed. "Yeah, it's perfect. Isn't it?"

We stood in respectful silence as I took in all the expensive furnishings and decor. Even the light fixtures looked like they had been lifted from a seventeenth century castle. If I hadn't already felt guilty about breaking into a dead woman's home, then I definitely felt bad about snooping around amidst all these priceless possessions.

The tabby took off decisively toward the right, and I followed. A short while later we wound up in the kitchen.

I eyed the beautiful white oak cabinetry appreciatively. Everything about this place proved larger than life. The giant island in the middle of the space was about the same size as a king bed, and the stainless-steel fridge appeared to be at least twice the size of my tiny rental's.

"Oh, good thinking," I murmured, unable to tear my eyes away from what had just become my own personal kitchen goals. "Since the food was prepared here, we should look for any proof of poisoning we can find."

At last I shifted my attention back to Octo-Cat. At least he didn't mind me moving slowly if it was to admire his former home.

In fact, he looked quite pleased with himself now. "Mmm-hmm. The Evian's in here."

I followed his gaze to the pantry where, sure enough, dozens of bottles of his preferred drinking water were stacked on the lowest shelf. "Do we really need to do this first?"

"Yes, now hurry. I'm parched." He lowered himself to the ground and waited.

I rolled my eyes but followed Octo-Cat's orders all the same. After I poured him the specified amount in the specified dish, I went back to the pantry and grabbed several bottles of water and a couple dozen cans of Fancy Feast to help get us through our time together. At least now I wouldn't have to spend a small fortune on Octo-Cat's shopping needs.

He lapped appreciatively from the dish and

then licked the outside of his mouth for good measure. "That hit the spot. Thanks."

I resisted the urge to tap my foot impatiently, which seemed the human equivalent of all his tail flicking. "Now that you're refreshed and rehydrated, perhaps you can show me around and help me see what you saw the night of the murder."

"Yes, okay." He crossed the kitchen at a slow, loping run, then jumped onto the counter.

I followed as he guided me toward the sink, which had been filled to the brim with dirty dishes.

"This is gross, but I'll do it for Ethel," he informed me before closing his eyes and sticking his nose into the middle of the mess.

He rooted around for a bit, then murmured, "It's this one."

I craned my neck but couldn't see what he meant. "Which one?"

"I'm pointing at it with my nose," came his muffled reply. "Please hurry, it's not the most pleasant smell."

One after the other, I pulled dirty plates from the sink. Each had a varying degree of salmon skin, rice grains, or butter glommed onto the surface, but I'd dealt with far worse than a couple day old dishes. The activity didn't bother me nearly as much as it did Octo-Cat.

"There. That's the one," he cried, slowly backing out of the sink and immediately licking his paw. "Smell it."

I did as he said but could only discern the faint smell of spoiled fish.

Octo-Cat rubbed his paw on top of his head, then brought it back down for more licks. "Now sniff another, and you'll see what I mean," he instructed.

I did as he said, making sure to take a good long whiff of each, but as far as I could tell they were no different. "What am I supposed to be smelling other than the fish?"

"Remember I told you about the funny smell?" He waited for me to nod, then revealed, "Only Ethel's plate had it."

"And this was her plate?" I asked, holding up the first for him to sniff again.

His face contorted in disgust. "Definitely."

"I don't know what I can do here. I can't smell the difference, and I wouldn't even know how to begin getting a forensics team on this."

"Tell them what I told you."

"Oh, sure. Tell them 'the cat told me.' That will

go over real well."

"I see your point." He stopped grooming and glanced around the kitchen. "Nothing looks out of order other than the mess from dinner. But open up the trash can and see if there's any poison in there."

I did as he said, stepping on the little foot pedal to raise the lid so we could both peer inside.

"Nothing," I told him with a shake of my head. "It's starting to look like she wasn't murdered, after all."

"Or that the culprit was smart enough to take the evidence with him. Besides, we have proof from the sink. It's not my fault your weak human nose refuses to smell what's right there in front of it."

I hated to admit it, but he was right. "Fine. Where else can we look for clues?"

He shook his head haughtily and flicked his tail to match. "First tell me you believe me about the murder."

"What? Why is that important?" I fixed him with my most domineering stare. I didn't think cats had alphas the way dogs do, but I needed some way to gain leverage here.

He growled, breaking my concentration. "If we're going to be working together, I need to know you believe in what we're doing. I need to know you'll do what it takes to get justice for Ethel."

I rolled my eyes and muttered, "Fine, I believe you."

"Next time, try a little harder to sound convincing." He sneered at me then jumped off the counter, shaking his little kitty booty as he strode away. "Seeing as you're the best option I've got, I'm just going to have to put up with you. C'mon, let me show you our bedroom."

While following him back to the entryway and up the grand staircase, I asked myself whether I did believe that Ethel had been murdered. I hadn't been able to see or smell any proof for myself just yet, but I also knew Octo-Cat well enough to know he wouldn't waste his time on false claims.

Whether or not it made much sense, he was convinced Ethel had met an unnatural end—and even though it made me more than a little crazy, I believed him.

CHAPTER SEVEN

I t felt strange standing in a room where someone had died less than forty-eight hours earlier. Even the air in Ethel Fulton's bedroom felt less oxygenated somehow, as if she'd tried to suck in every last breath she could before taking her last. At that lovely thought, I shuddered and wrapped my arms around myself.

Octo-Cat hopped up on the bed and pawed at the comforter. "This is where she died. I slept on this pillow here, and she slept on the side closest to the bathroom. Usually she got up a couple times per night to pollute her water bowl. You humans are a disgusting bunch, by the way, but I loved Ethel and was able to overlook her flaws."

"Your point?" I asked with a sigh.

He raised a lip at me but kept his hiss to himself. "That night she didn't wake up at all. It was the first sign I knew something was definitely wrong."

I hovered awkwardly near the bed, unwilling to sit down or even to touch it. "I thought the funny smelling food was the first sign something was wrong."

My companion sniffed around the bed as if in search of something specific. "That's when I first suspected, but when she didn't get up at night, I knew for sure."

I gave Octo-Cat a few uninterrupted moments to finish his investigation of the bed. When he settled back on his pillow, I said, "Okay, so even though this is where she died, I don't think it has anything to do with the murder. Downstairs there were six dinner plates. Assuming one was for Ethel, can you remember who any of the other five guests were?"

"I might be able to identify them if I saw them again, and more likely by smell than sight."

I contemplated this. Octo-Cat's heightened sense of smell was of no use to me. The only other person I'd ever be able to identify by scent would be

Bethany from work—and that was only because of her essential oils obsession. At that, an encouraging thought struck me. "Were any of them at the will reading this morning?"

He yawned and stretched his paws in front of himself in some kind of sleek yoga pose. "Yes, all of them were there," he revealed.

Suddenly, solving this thing seemed not only possible, but likely. Trying not to startle Octo-Cat with my sudden burst of eagerness, I said, "But you don't know which one killed Ethel?"

"No, none of them had the funny smell from the dinner party when I saw them this morning," he confided with a frown.

"And you don't remember their names?"

Octo-Cat shook his head.

Forgetting my earlier disgust, I sighed and sunk down onto the mattress beside him, feeling all the wind leave my newly raised sails. "Seeing as there were at least twenty people at the reading, we have quite a few suspects."

He sighed, too. "Yes, it would seem we do."

I shivered upon realizing that I was sitting in the exact same spot where old lady Fulton had died not even two full days earlier. "Maybe if we try to—"

"Hush!" Octo-Cat yelled, leaping to attention. His ears twitched like tiny satellite dishes trying to find the best reception. "Someone just came in the house."

My stomach dropped past my feet and straight through the floor boards. *"What?"*

He listened a little bit longer. "Yes, someone is definitely inside."

Knowing my luck, it would be the killer, coming to scrub the scene clean of any lingering evidence— evidence I'd been too stupid to actually locate. Now it would be gone forever, and poor Ethel Fulton would have to go into the afterlife unavenged. Not to mention if the killer found us, he just might strike again—and, of course, we stood right in his path.

"We need to get out of here," I mouthed, hoping Octo-Cat could read lips.

He jumped onto the floor and trotted out through the bedroom door which I'd foolishly left wide open.

I listened for what felt like an eternity, waiting for someone to cross paths with my hapless sidekick. Would Octo-Cat recognize the danger? And, if so, would he find a way to alert me to it?

Several minutes passed without any sign of

Octo-Cat or anyone else. Taking a deep breath, I tiptoed out into the hallway and toward the grand staircase. I just had to make it down these steps and out the door, then I never had to set sight on this place again.

Although I did a great job of descending quietly, I did it at the expense of a speedy getaway.

About halfway down, a shadowy figure appeared in the foyer and paused upon noticing me.

Of all the things I could have done then, I chose the worst possible one. I froze in place.

"Who's there?" the figure asked. The voice clearly belonged to a woman, which eased my fears a bit. I'd have a hard time defending myself against a full-grown man, but at five foot eight and a size twelve, I could probably fight off most other women… unless she had a weapon.

"I… I'm…" How could I possibly explain my trespassing? The truth about the talking cat and our murder investigation would be worse than pretty much any lie, but I was far too frightened to think up a good lie on the spot.

Luckily, Octo-Cat chose that exact moment to come in through his electronic cat door and race up the stairs to join me. "Tell her you're looking for my food and bed and other supplies," he commanded.

Oh, that was a great idea. It was also at least partially true.

"I'm watching the cat for a few days and came over to pick up his things. Wh-who are you?" I asked boldly, standing tall as if I had every right to be here.

She stepped back and flicked a switch that illuminated the overhead chandelier, casting light over us both. "Obviously you're not close with the family or you wouldn't have to ask that. So why don't you start by telling me who *you* are?"

"She's bluffing," Octo-Cat whispered at my side. "She's just as scared as you are. She's throwing out human stress hormones like crazy."

"I work for Mr. Fulton." I descended a few steps, keeping my eyes trained on the other woman. "Should I tell him you stopped by?"

"Nice one," Octo-Cat cheered behind me.

The woman cursed under her breath. The deep bags beneath her eyes implied she hadn't slept well in nights, and the way she twisted her mouth into a frown told me I had her outwitted.

"No, he wouldn't like that," she mumbled,

glancing behind her then back up toward me. "Look, I'm not taking anything. Just looking over Aunt Ethel's things to make sure I don't get taken when divvying up the inheritance. I'm on my way out, though, so no harm done." She lifted her hands in surrender and waited for me to join her on the main floor.

"I suppose I don't need to tell Mr. Fulton about this, but we had both better leave and lock up," I said with far more courage than I felt.

"Yes, okay." She backed away slowly, keeping her eyes on me the whole time, then bumbled for the doorknob and swung the front door open so forcefully it slammed against the wall. If I wasn't suspicious before, then I definitely questioned her motives now.

"See you around, then," the woman said, peering through the door one last time before scurrying down the steps.

I watched as she got into an old car and sat mumbling to herself behind the wheel. Even though she was on her way now, it didn't mean that she—or others—wouldn't be back soon. I had to get out of there, but first I needed to grab Octo-Cat's things from the kitchen.

He followed me at a quick clip. "You did great,"

he said. "I'm starting to think that maybe you're up to this task after all."

"Gee, thanks," I told him as I packed my arms with the Evian and cat food cans as best I could. "Mind watching my back in case she tries to sneak up and stab me while I'm not looking?"

Octo-Cat jumped on the counter and widened his eyes. "Oh, she's not the killer."

"What makes you so sure?" I mumbled, struggling with my off balanced load. "Was she not there that night?"

"Oh, she was there, but she's not smart enough to commit a murder, let alone conceal it. Believe me, that's Ethel's niece. She's, hands down, the stupidest human I've ever met. She couldn't have concocted this."

"It almost sounds like you admire the killer," I whispered while leaving the kitchen. I didn't know whether the other visitor had left yet or whether she would return before I had a chance to make my getaway.

My companion hissed. "No, believe me, I'm mad as a human without its cell phone. I just know she doesn't have it in her. That still leaves four other guests that could have done it, though."

The front door still hung wide open, but the

other woman's car had disappeared from the drive. Thank goodness, because I wasn't up for more small talk even if I could rest assured that it wouldn't end with my own murder.

"But you don't know who any of the other guests were? Earlier you said you didn't know anyone, but you seemed to recognize Ethel's niece right away."

He sighed as if he were the one suffering a fool here. "It's scent memory. Some details don't click into place without it."

"I've never heard of such a ridiculous thing." I watched my feet as we picked our way across the uneven ground to the side of the house where I'd concealed my car near a copse of tall trees.

"Well, how many cats did you have deep conversations with before you met me?"

I had to admit, he had me there. "Point taken. But this little field trip accomplished nothing, so what are we supposed to do next?"

We reached my car and I set my load of cans and bottles on the ground so I could open the trunk and stash everything inside.

"It definitely was *not* nothing." Octo-Cat jumped onto the hood of my car and looked down on me as if I were a peasant and he was king. "We got my food and Evian, didn't we?"

I shook my head and chuckled as I slammed the trunk closed again. We'd come face to face with danger but were still nowhere near solving our murder mystery. At least we had Evian, though!

CHAPTER EIGHT

The next morning, I woke up to an ear-piercing cry in the wee hours. The room was still shrouded in darkness, so I groped for my phone to serve as a makeshift flashlight.

"Ack, right in my eye!" Octo-Cat shouted as he jumped from the bed to the floor to escape the path of the light.

I struggled to sit, my limbs still heavy with sleep. "What's going on? What's wrong?"

He turned to face me. His glinting eyes widened as they adjusted to my flashlight. "It's time for breakfast," he informed me.

A quick glance at my phone confirmed that it was only five o'clock, more than two full hours before I generally awoke on a work day.

"No way, not going to happen," I moaned and pulled the covers over my head. "Go away."

That same horrible banshee cry sounded again, sending shivers up my spine and digging straight into my brain.

"Is that you?" I hissed.

Octo-Cat hissed back but otherwise kept his voice slow and at its normal volume. "It's breakfast time," he repeated. "If I could open the can myself, I would, but I can't. So, get up and use those opposable thumbs the way God intended, darling."

"Fine, but I hate you," I whined as I threw my legs over the side of the bed. He had me up, but that didn't mean I needed to hurry.

He ran ahead and turned several circles while waiting for me to catch up. "The feeling is mutual. At least until I've had my breakfast."

"And me, my coffee," I said, shuddering as I remembered yesterday's run-in with the office coffeemaker. Perhaps I would switch to tea going forward.

In the kitchen I plunked his favorite congealed salmon pâté onto a plate and set it on the ground for my spoiled roommate. *"Bon Appetit,"* I mumbled, shuffling back toward my bedroom.

I didn't even have a chance to lie back down

before Octo-Cat took a swipe at my feet and growled. "No, you can't go back to bed. It's morning and I need to have my breakfast."

"I just fed you. Go eat already and leave me alone." I dropped into bed and turned on my side so that I wouldn't have to look at his demanding kitty face.

"Why is this so hard to understand?" he said with a sigh, his whiskers twitching furiously. "I can't eat unless you stand nearby and watch me. Maybe tell me what a good cat I am, too."

"But you're not a good cat," I grumbled. Right now he was pretty much the worst cat in the world. After all, none of the others were rousing me from sleep at this unholy hour.

"Ethel always petted me and talked to me while I ate. Please, don't you think…?" His words broke away and despite my better judgment I turned to look straight into his huge, pleading eyes.

"Fine!" I sputtered. "But tomorrow we wake up on my schedule."

Octo-Cat didn't say anything as he led the way back to my kitchen, his tail held high and hips swaying in a way that definitely looked put on for my benefit.

"Oh, great and mighty Octo-Cat, you are such

a good kitty," I said, rolling my eyes as he took his first tentative bite of that awful-smelling breakfast.

"Hey, what did I tell you about calling me 'kitty?'" He grumbled between bites. "But I've gotta say, the other thing is growing on me."

"What? *Octo-Cat?*" I regarded him suspiciously. This was a surprise given how he'd stubbornly insisted on his ridiculously long moniker until now.

"That's the one," he confirmed with a smack of his lips as he continued to gobble up Fancy Feast.

"It suits you."

"And it makes me seem hip and modern, too."

"Oh, yes, you're one cool cat." Maybe it was time to teach the poor guy some new slang. After all, he'd taken all his current lingo from a woman in her eighties.

When he finished his meal, I poured some Evian into a mug and set it before Octo-Cat. He lapped it up appreciatively and then began the first of his many daily grooming ministrations.

"Since I'm up, I guess I'll go get ready," I informed him, thanking my lucky stars when he didn't follow me into the bathroom. I was able to take a shower without any added drama.

The hot water pounded my skin, slowly bringing me back to life. By the time I finished my own grooming rituals, I found myself in a much better mood.

"Good to see you've finally woken up," Octo-Cat said with an approving nod. "What time do we head into the office?"

"We? No, no, no. There's no way I can justify taking you into the firm."

"But I was there yesterday," he argued with a child-like pout.

"For the will reading."

"Well, just have another will reading then. Besides, if I'm there, I can help suss out the killer."

I crossed my arms over my chest and stared him down without blinking. "You're *not* coming."

He ran toward the door, calling to me in a sing-song voice. "Too bad you can't stop me."

Oh, what a brat. Leave it to Octo-Cat to always want to be at the center of all the action. He was really quite outgoing as far as cats were concerned. If I had any chance of leaving him at home, then I needed to come up with something important for him to do here—or at least something I could trick him into thinking was important.

What was that saying about curiosity and cats again? I was banking on it being true.

"I'm only going to work because I haven't got a

choice in the matter," I informed him. "You, however, do. And it would be much better if you stayed here and did some research into our case."

He flicked his tail, but otherwise looked intrigued. Score one for clichéd old sayings. "Oh? Well, what did you have in mind?"

If I took too long to think, Octo-Cat would figure me out so I went with the first thing that popped into my mind. "Research. On the Internet."

"I can't type," he said with a scowl. "Or read, for that matter."

"Can't read?" I don't know why I was surprised. Most cats didn't talk. Maybe I'd just assumed that Octo-Cat could do all things like my very own super kitty sidekick.

He abandoned the door and joined me in the living room. "Until I met you, I had no idea humans had such a complex system of communication," he explained. "Your different sounds mean different things! I always thought it was just about emotion, but you actually seem to assign noises to various objects and concepts. It's fascinating."

"Right back at you, cat." It still hadn't ceased to amaze me that Octo-Cat thought of humans as just another animal. In his mind, cats were the most intellectually superior species on the planet, which seemed laughable to me. Were humans otherwise deluded about their place in the animal kingdom? It sure made me wonder.

I'd been wondering something else, too, and decided to ask Octo-Cat about it. "So, you're not speaking English?"

He twitched his whiskers in confusion. "What's English? Is that your word for human? Because no, I'm not speaking human. You're speaking cat."

"I'm not speaking cat, though." At least I was pretty sure I wasn't speaking in a series of meows, purrs, and growls.

"And yet somehow we understand each other." Octo-Cat looked bored, even though I found the intricacies of our communication amazingly interesting. Maybe at the end of the day curiosity killed the human, too.

We sat in companionable silence as we both puzzled over this, one of us more than the other.

At last I said, "I suppose that's another mystery we'll have to figure out. You know, once we solve the more pressing murder mystery."

"There's no mystery about it," he informed me, his eyes flashing with untold knowledge. "It's magic."

"Magic?" I laughed at this notion. "You believe in magic?"

"You don't?" He looked authentically surprised at this.

How much did we humans not know about the rest of the world? I was beginning to think it was substantial. I'd look into this all later. Right now, I needed to focus on distracting him so that I could slip away to the office, unaccompanied.

"Okay, so that's what you can do for me," I told him, reaching forward to grab the remote from the coffee table. "I'll leave the TV on for you and you can learn to read human."

"Eww, why?"

"So you can help me with the research, of course."

"Are you going to learn cat?" he shot back.

"Sure, you can give me some lessons once I'm home from work." I agreed primarily to avoid an argument but had to admit, the idea of learning such an uncharted new language did excite me.

The TV flickered to life at the press of the button and immediately our eyes darted to the screen. After a bit of channel surfing, I settled on one of the kids' channels where a caramel-skinned little girl and her monkey talked directly to the viewer. I pressed a series of buttons, at last reaching the option to enable subtitles.

Octo-Cat meowed right back at the screen, immediately enamored of the program. I watched with him for a few minutes, then managed to slip out undetected just as I'd hoped.

I'd be painfully early to the office that day, but maybe that would be to my benefit. Little by little, a plan began to form in my mind.

Yes, today would be a productive day when it came to solving Ethel Fulton's murder. If all went according to plan, I might even be able to discover the culprit before returning home in the evening.

CHAPTER NINE

On my way to the office, I stopped by the local coffee shop to order lattes for the partners and all the associates. Even though I couldn't really afford it, I needed an excuse to talk to everyone and see what I could learn about the will reading and Ethel Fulton's purported cause of death.

Thankfully, no matter how much Nan wanted me to be a fully functional adult, she would still step in whenever I couldn't make rent. Generally, my pocket money went toward books or community college courses or online webinars, but I figured Octo-Cat's and my mystery would keep me too busy to spend much time on recreational learning for the next few days.

I'd read enough police procedural novels by this point to know it took a fair bit of work to identify a killer. Surely in the real world, many cases proved to be open and shut, but I doubted Ethel's would turn out that way.

For starters, all of my evidence was based on hearsay... *from a cat.*

And even though I believed him, I couldn't exactly use his word to justify myself to others. Octo-Cat had also given me just enough to legitimize his claims of murder, but not enough to guide my questioning when talking to anyone else.

All of this meant I'd need to keep myself casual and conversational while trying to glean information from my boss and coworkers. The surprise coffee delivery would be my way in, but I'd need to rely on my wits to learn anything of actual value.

Oh boy, I definitely had my work cut out for me.

Thanks to my rude awakening that morning, I reached work a full hour before my normal start time. Only two other cars stood in the parking lot— Mr. Fulton's and Bethany's. So much for all the extra lattes. I just hoped I'd be able to secretly warm them in the microwave later without anyone noticing.

Trying not to show my disappointment, I

floated into the office with my oversized tray of coffees and a bright smile on my face.

"Good morning," I sang, passing by the front desk where I normally sat to greet any visitors who happened to drop by the firm.

Only silence greeted me.

"Hello?" I called, knowing for a fact I'd seen their cars. As I moved down the hall toward Mr. Fulton's office, I flicked on the overhead lights.

"Mr. Fulton?"

The door opened abruptly, causing me to jump back. Thank goodness the hot coffees didn't spill down my front or I'd have found myself in the hospital with a wicked work injury a second day in a row.

Once I regained my balance, I glanced up at my boss. The poor man was almost unrecognizable. Mr. Fulton appeared almost comically disheveled. His normally well-pressed shirt was wrinkled, and his tie hung askew. His eyes focused on the ground, meaning it took him an extra moment to realize I was standing right in front of him.

"Good morning, sir," I said carefully. "Is... Is everything okay?"

He glanced up at me and plastered on a polite

91

smile, which I saw right through. "Oh, yes. Yes, I'm fine. Is this coffee for me?"

After I handed him a latte, he retreated back into his office and slammed the door behind him without so much as a *thank you*, a *good morning*, or an *I'm glad you didn't die at the hands of that coffeemaker yesterday*.

Strange. Definitely strange.

Shrugging it off, I headed toward Bethany's office next. The room sat dark and quiet even though I could have sworn I'd seen her car in the lot, too. Maybe I really had lost my mind, or maybe it was everyone else who had gone crazy.

Either way, I had the strange feeling of being watched. Did the killer know I was on to him, or was some other dark danger looming?

Danger, *phfff.* I was just being silly.

It was still my plain, old boring office, only a little bit earlier in the day. Mr. Fulton had just lost a relative and had a complicated estate to manage as well, so of course, he was out of sorts.

As for Bethany, she often liked to escape outside to grab some fresh air, which also made sense seeing as a chemical fog hung in her office from more than a year of overzealous essential oil use. In fact, she was probably hanging around in the yard now, which would give me the perfect opportunity to talk with her in private before the others arrived.

Having talked myself down from that near fright, I set the tray of coffees on my desk, grabbed one for me and one for Bethany, then headed outside. I took a lap around the entire building, but only found a shifty looking squirrel staring at me suspiciously.

Where could Bethany have gone?

Returning to the parking lot, I glanced into her car, but it also stood empty. When I turned around, I caught a flash of gray disappearing behind the building.

"Bethany?" I called, jogging after.

But again, nothing was there.

Giving up at last, I went back inside and found Bethany waiting for me beside my desk. "How did you…?"

"What?" she asked, pawing at one of the coffees before at last picking it up and holding it between her two hands awkwardly. "I was here the whole time," she offered with a shrug when I didn't say anything more. If that was true, then it meant she was more than likely in Mr. Fulton's office with him. Her office had definitely been empty, and none of the others had been opened yet for the day.

But why the secrecy?

Had I stumbled upon a new mystery altogether?

No, Mr. Fulton would never have an affair. Not in a million years. And especially not with harsh and brassy Bethany, who was so much his wife's opposite. Thanks to Octo-Cat, my imagination had run away with me, plain and simple.

Now it was time to stop speculating about my coworkers and start gathering intel about Ethel's murder. Seeing as Bethany was already a tad harried, maybe she would slip and tell me more than she would have otherwise intended.

I had to give it a shot.

"So…" I said, setting one of the coffees down and taking a small sip of the other. "Yesterday was crazy, huh?"

Her face jerked toward me as if she'd only just remembered I was there, and then a serpentine smile slithered across her face. "Seriously crazy," she agreed.

"Did you miss much because of taking me to the hospital?"

"Oh, no. I don't think so. When I got back, they'd only just made it to the part about the cat." She tucked her light blonde hair behind her ears and offered me a placating smile.

"I heard Ethel left a lot of her estate to Oct... I mean, her cat. That really had everyone up in arms, I bet."

She settled into our conversation, becoming less stiff as we gossiped. "How would you feel if you'd been denied your inheritance because of a common house cat?"

"I hear he's part Maine Coon," I said, wondering why I felt the need to defend a cat I'd known less than twenty-four hours and didn't really even like all that much, anyway. Bethany was right. I still didn't know how much Octo-Cat had inherited, but judging from the house we visited yesterday, it had to be a pretty penny, indeed.

"Well, whatever the case," she said with a frown. "I don't think that woman is going to be remembered favorably after this. At least not by her family."

"Did they like her before?" I wondered aloud, trying not to show my rapt interest in her answer as we finally got to the meat of this juicy tidbit.

Bethany shrugged. "Who knows?"

When she turned to walk away, I blurted out the first thing that popped into my head. "Do you know how she died?" I practically shouted. "Is it possible someone in the family, you know, helped her along to get a shot at their inheritance early?"

Bethany froze in place. A few awkward seconds passed before she burst out laughing. "Really, Angie? It seems you've been watching a bit too much TV. People die every day. Very few of them are murdered."

I forced a chuckle, too. "Oh, you're right. I stayed up late reading last night and then woke up early because of the cat. I'm afraid my brain is a bit fried."

She seemed interested in this. "The cat. Yes, you took him in, didn't you?"

"Yup, I wanted to help the family during this difficult time, and this seemed like the easiest way."

Bethany stalked back toward me with slow, deliberate steps. Dropping her voice to a husky rasp, she whispered, "You better be glad those murder mysteries are only in your head, because whoever gets the cat gets the money. If he stays with you too much longer, you could be next on the killer's list."

A chill crept from my fingertips all the way to my heart, and the little hairs on the back of my neck also stood tall and on alert. I was just about to ask what she was insinuating when Bethany exploded in laughter once again.

"You should have seen your face," she crowed, turning on heel and strolling back to her office. Her laughter bobbed along after her, leaving me alone with my mostly full tray of coffees.

If I hadn't known better, I'd swear Bethany was trying to get a rise out of me—or extend a warning. Did she know something I didn't? Could she be at least partially to blame?

Suddenly I didn't feel so safe anymore.

CHAPTER TEN

About half an hour later, the other attorneys began to trickle in to the office. By then I'd already decided I would never show up early ever again. Mr. Thompson sent me out for coffee when he arrived, but at least this time he gave me the cash to cover my purchase.

When I returned with a fresh tray of hot beverages in hand, I found Diane Fulton sitting in the small waiting area with a magazine folded over her crossed legs.

"Oh, there you are, Angie," she said, turning to me with an exacerbated smile. "Good morning."

"Good morning," I responded hesitantly, shifting my weight from one foot to the other. Normally I loved Diane's visits, but today her presence had me nervous considering her husband's oddball behavior that morning and my suspicions of a possible affair.

I put on a huge fake smile of my own. "Is there something I can help you with?"

Her hands shook in her lap, belying the extreme emotion she was trying so hard to keep buried beneath the surface. "Well, I came in to see my husband, but he doesn't seem to be around. I figured if I waited long enough for you to return maybe you'd know where I can find him."

"I'm sorry, no. If he's not in his office, I'm not sure where he would have gone." I hesitated again before asking, "Is everything okay?"

Diane tucked her normally neat hair behind her ears and swallowed hard. It was only then I noticed how disheveled she appeared, too. Rather than her usual wardrobe of trendy designer blouses and skirts, she wore an old T-shirt that had a large, blotchy stain across the chest. She'd paired that monstrosity with track pants and flip flops, neither of which I ever would have guessed she even owned, let alone would ever be seen wearing in public.

I set the coffees on a side table and stooped down to talk to my friend, who now visibly had to work to fight back tears. "You can always talk to me," I cooed, wondering if I should offer a tissue or a hug.

"It's Richard," she confessed with a sob. "He didn't come home last night, and he's not answering any of my calls or texts. I don't know what to do."

I thought back to that morning. I'd never seen my boss so out of sorts, and I was willing to bet Diane had never seen him lose his composure like this either.

"Tell you what," I said, hoping I wouldn't regret this. "I'll shoot you a call whenever I next see him."

Her eyes widened, the unshed tears now sparkling with mirth. "Oh, would you? That would be such a huge help."

"Sure." I really didn't want to insert myself into the middle of their domestic drama but also couldn't ignore my friend in her hour of need.

"He's been acting so strange this past week," Diane continued after grabbing a tissue for herself and giving her nose a good blow. "We've been married almost thirty years, but suddenly it's like he's a stranger."

I really didn't know what to say to that, so I patted her on the shoulder and offered a placating smile. "There, there, I'm sure everything is fine.

He's going through a rough time with the death of his aunt. Right?"

Diane nodded. "Ethel was always my favorite in the family. I just wished we would have spent more time with her in the final days. I think we all half expected her to live forever. It's been such a shock."

I would have loved to ask her about the dinner party, but there was no way I could justify having that knowledge. Instead I said, "I really am so sorry for your loss."

She sniffed and tucked the used tissue into her purse. "Oh, look at me. I'm keeping you from your work." She tossed the magazine back on the coffee table and stood, attempting and failing to brush the wrinkles from her outfit. She laughed sarcastically. "I'm such a mess. Maybe a salon day is in order."

"That sounds like the perfect idea to me."

"You promise you'll call me if you see him?"

"I promise." That at least I could do. Solving the murder, though? I was seriously beginning to worry about what other unsavory secrets I might uncover if I kept digging.

Diane nodded, glanced around the office, and then surprised me with a tight hug. "Thank you, Angie. You have no idea how much you've helped."

Less than a minute later, she was gone and I was just as confused as ever.

Our youngest associate, Derek, emerged from the office he shared with another of our blue blood frat-type attorneys in training, Brad, and made a beeline straight for the coffee. "Thanks for this," he said, grabbing two and spinning on his heel to dive back into their office.

I followed sitting at the corner of Derek's desk, so neither man could ignore me. "You guys were at the will reading yesterday, right?"

Derek took a slow slurp of coffee. "I wasn't invited, but Brad was." He didn't seem too happy about this fact, but I didn't have time to unpack Derek's feelings when there was still so much more to learn about the Fultons.

I fixed my gaze on Brad and tried to show my interest in the topic without encouraging any flirtations on his part. "I've heard the craziest things. What happened?"

He spun in his chair with a self-satisfied smirk. "Well, there was this hot secretary who got electrocuted and had to be rushed to the hospital."

Non-detective me would have either slapped him knowing full well I could lose my job for doing so, or she would have stormed out without so much as a second glance. Brad had asked me out once or twice or a few dozen times, and each time I'd said no. I would forever say no, that was one certainty I'd happily stake my life on.

Add to all this the fact he referred to me as the firm's secretary on a regular basis, and I was more than a little irked. I was a paralegal. Just because I happened to bring everyone coffee most days didn't change that. Besides, I was pretty sure Brad had only scraped by in law school because of his father's connections. Everything I had career-wise—which admittedly wasn't much—came from my own merits.

I forced a smile. "After that, I mean?" As skeezy as I found Brad to be, at least I could count on him wanting to impress me. That meant he might be a little looser with his tongue than some of the more tight-lipped attorneys. And that's exactly what I was banking on now.

He cleared his throat and adjusted his tie, sitting straighter in his seat as he revealed, "The old lady left almost everything to her cat. And one lady lost her cool completely when she heard."

Oh, now we're getting somewhere!

"What lady?" I asked, quirking an eyebrow in curiosity.

His face contorted in a grimace. "She was short, had gray hair, pretty frumpy. I think maybe it was the niece?"

Hmm, that sure sounded a lot like the person Octo-Cat and I found lurking around Ethel's estate the night before. "What did she do when she found out?"

"She started yelling all these profanities, said how much she had looked after Ethel over the years while all the cat ever did was catch some mice and poop in a box. She said *she* deserved the money."

I laughed and silently tucked away the second-hand insult to deliver to Octo-Cat later. "And what did everyone else say?"

"Basically, to stay in her lane. She sat down and shut up pretty quickly after that, then rushed out of there as fast as her feet could carry her when it was over."

I chuckled and tried my best to picture the fiasco. "Sounds like I missed quite the show."

Brad popped to his feet and popped his collar in a move I'm sure he thought was sexy, but I found ridiculously clownish. "I'd be happy to give you a recap over dinner."

I yawned and shook my head. "Thanks, but I'll have to pass."

He shrugged off the bruise to his ego. I was beginning to believe he had freaky healing powers like the Wolverine or the cheerleader girl from *Heroes*. Nothing ever seemed to faze him more than as a glancing blow.

"See you guys later," I said with a polite nod to Derek, whom I'd always liked far more than Brad. Then again, I liked everyone in the office better than Brad. Except maybe Bethany. Those two were probably tied for last place on my list of favorite coworkers.

Maybe if she wasn't having an affair with Mr. Fulton, she'd consider Brad a possible suitor instead. That would be great for getting him off my case, but I wasn't sure if it would be worth the nightmare possibility of those two teaming up.

When I passed back through the main area, I noticed all the to-go cups of coffee had been claimed while I chatted with Brad and Derek about yesterday's will reading. That meant either someone was being greedy or that Mr. Fulton was indeed nearby and had consciously hidden from his wife during her visit.

I took a deep breath before going to check his office. Nobody responded to my knock, but the door hadn't been latched all the way, so I gently pushed my way inside. I knew it was wrong to snoop, but it was also wrong to murder—and I needed to at least try to bring the culprit to justice.

After my strange run-in first with Mr. Fulton and then with his wife, I was beginning to suspect my kindly boss could have blood on his hands, which made breaking into his office even riskier.

I moved slowly through the space, ready to bolt at the first sign of danger—or of Mr. Fulton's return. At first everything appeared normal, but then a swath of bright purple lying in a heap under his desk caught my eye. Wheeling the chair back, I bent down for a closer look.

And came face-to-cup with a frilly silk bra. It was way fancier than anything I would ever wear, and too sexy for Diane. Could that mean…?

I didn't want to believe the worst about my boss, but I was already beginning to suspect him of murder, so maybe adultery wasn't too far a stretch by comparison.

As easy as it would be to peg this whole thing on the most obvious and immediate suspect, I still had a hard time picturing my favorite boss as the killer of a kindly old cat lady.

It just didn't make any sense. He'd always seemed like such a nice guy even, and perhaps especially, for a lawyer. Had it all been a ruse to lull us all into overlooking his culpability?

But why now?

Why would he kill his aunt? Was it cold and calculated or more of a passion thing? It sure seemed that slipping poison into someone's dinner was something you planned in advance. If he'd really done this horrible thing—had slowly and surely carried it out—then why did he seem so frazzled now?

I just couldn't figure it out, but one thing was for sure: I needed to get out of there before I was caught purple-handed with this newfound evidence. Sure, what exactly it was evidence for remained to be seen, but soon the truth about everything would come out.

Yes, even if I had to force it.

CHAPTER ELEVEN

I didn't see Mr. Fulton for the rest of the day, which only raised my suspicions that much more. Diane called just before the end of my shift to check in, and I absolutely hated disappointing her with my lack of news.

On the drive home, I rolled down my windows and let the cool ocean breeze sweep through my car. It was really quite nice to be able to drive without claws stuck into my thighs for a change. And, speaking of claws, I really hoped Octo-Cat hadn't made a disaster of my house while I was away.

A few short minutes later I pulled into the gravel lot of my rental, sucked in as much fresh air as I could, and entered expecting the worst.

Octo-Cat greeted me at the door by rubbing against my pant leg and shaking his tail. "You were gone forever!"

I thought about bending down to pet him but didn't want to spoil his mood so soon after returning. "Just a little longer than my normal nine to five. Not forever," I explained.

"Nine to five? Sounds like a prison sentence to me." He had a point; I could give him that.

"Yeah, well, you're not exactly wrong," I admitted with a weary sigh.

"Then why do you go?" He sat down and studied me without hissing, flicking his tail, or otherwise expressing displeasure. Had he been body-snatched while I was away? This was definitely not the crabby tabby I'd come to know and loathe.

I rubbed my index finger and thumb together. "It's all about the Benjamins, babe. And what's this? You actually missed me?" I didn't want to risk turning him back into a striped version of Grumpy Cat, but I had to know.

He shrugged. "I like knowing you're nearby. You know, in case I need some fresh Evian or help with a particularly tricky hairball."

That made me laugh. "Thank goodness you survived."

He grinned like… well, like the Cheshire cat, then informed me, "Speaking of which, it's time for my supper."

I saluted him and headed for the kitchen. After I plopped a fresh chunk of pâté down for him and filled a cup with Evian, I proceeded to tell him what a good cat he was, just as I'd been instructed earlier that day.

When he finished his evening meal, he jumped up onto the counter and said, "Well done. You may pet me now."

"Um, okay." It felt strangely intimate to run my fingers through his brown and black fur and rub him all the way from the top of his head down to the base of his tail. It felt even stranger to hear him purr.

"You're welcome," he said after a few more strokes. "I know you've been wanting to do that for a while, and—*hey*—you've earned it. But please stop now or I will have to bite you."

I yanked my hand away faster than you could say, "Oh, brother." Then I said it aloud anyway for good measure.

Octo-Cat hopped back onto the floor and guided me into the living room where my TV still sat tuned in to the kid's channel I'd selected for him earlier that day. "Did you learn a lot today?" I asked with a smirk.

He yawned and nodded. "In between napping, yes."

"Aren't you going to ask me about my day?" I was eager to hear his thoughts about Mr. Fulton's strange behavior coupled with the fact that he seemed to have gone missing.

"The thought hadn't occurred to me," he admitted with another yawn. "Besides, I still have so much more to tell you about mine."

"Oh, I'm sorry. Please go ahead." I took a seat on the couch and motioned for him to regale me with all the many, varied events that had filled his day. It was the least I could do after he'd managed not to wreck everything I owned in some kind of irrational hissy fit as I had expected.

He jumped onto the coffee table and paced back and forth, speaking rapidly as he recounted his day. "First I woke up hungry as I often do. It took me a while to get you out of bed, and even longer to teach you how to properly serve me my morning repast. All in all, I'd give you a C for effort. Average, but not special."

"Okay, great. Can we skip ahead please?" I asked in irritation. I'd never met someone who could turn on a dime as quickly as this cat. One moment he lovingly greets me at the door and the next he's back to insulting me. This inconsistency seemed to be a staple of his character. At least I could trust him to always tell me exactly what was on his mind. That had to count for something, especially when it came to solving a murder mystery.

Octo-Cat continued to pace back and forth, speaking in rhythm with his quick steps. "After you left, I watched the cartoon girl solve mysteries using the items in her backpack. We should really get a backpack to help with our case, too. Oh, and a map."

I chuckled, which apparently was the wrong response.

"I'm dead serious here," he said, his amber eyes boring into my blues. "I also learned about pineapples under the sea and other oddities of the human world. I'm understanding your language a bit better, but you as a species a lot less. Why broadcast shows about a sea sponge and his pet snail? Why not focus on your own species, or at least a superior species like the *Felis catus?*"

"Um, I don't really have an answer to that one.

People do weird things all the time, like commit murder or have affairs. You'll never believe what I discovered today at work."

"Oh, I'm sure I will believe it. You humans are also quite predictable," he informed me, plopping his rear down on the coffee table and wagging his tail ominously. "But first I must tell you about the rest of my day."

There was *more?* How much more could there possibly be?

I really wasn't looking forward to a blow by blow of all the cartoons he'd watched that day, especially not when we had far more important matters to discuss. Still, it seemed important to him that I give him my undivided attention, so I leaned back into the couch cushions and motioned for him to continue.

"At first I tried napping on the back of the couch, but I found it too lumpy for my liking. After scouring the premises, I found the perfect spot where a patch of light landed on the carpet and warmed it nicely. I napped there for roughly an hour before the sun moved, rendering the spot unsatisfactory."

He waited for me to say something, so I settled for, "Of course."

Pleased, he continued, "Then I went to your bedroom and found a nice twist in the comforter where I made something of a burrow. Unfortunately, I was unable to jump down in time when I woke up with a hairball clogging my windpipe. So, you may want to do a load of laundry before turning in for the night."

He puked on my comforter? *Gross.* At least he'd told me rather than letting me discover it for myself. Thank goodness for small miracles.

"When you came home, you fed me, and this time you made a much better showing of it. I'll give it an *A minus,* I think. Now we are here. How the rest of the day unfolds remains to be seen."

"Sounds like you had a busy day," I summarized sarcastically.

He winked at me, not catching the humor. "Yes, it was a good day, considering."

I considered asking him what he meant by that, but decided I'd rather not get in another long conversation about the intricacies of daily cat life when we still needed to discuss what I'd stumbled across at work. "May I tell you about mine?"

"It will be hard to top my day, but you may try."

I thought this meant he was happy with me, and for some reason that made my heart swell with pride. Maybe like Brad, I craved affection from someone who didn't easily offer it. Octo-Cat's kindness felt like a reward that I had earned for good behavior, and I was lapping it right up.

Without going into too much detail—because I knew how easy it was to lose his interest—I recapped the events of my day, ending with the purple bra I'd discovered in Mr. Fulton's office.

Octo-Cat shook his head. "And humans think we're the ones who need to be neutered. At least the only thing we do is make kittens, not trouble."

I had to agree with him there. "Does it surprise you that Mr. Fulton could be having an affair?"

"Not really, but I don't know him well and I don't understand your human marriages, anyway. Those tiny collars you wear on your fingers… It's like being micro-chipped, right? You can try to run away, but they'll always find you again and bring you home. Frustrating."

"Something like that," I said, trying to hide my smile. "Do you think Mr. Fulton could have been the one to poison Ethel?"

Octo-Cat thought about this for a good long time. "He's the one with gray hair and extra padding, right?"

Mr. Fulton was fit and slim, and most of his hair

was still brown. Something wasn't adding up. "Are you talking about the woman we saw at your house yesterday?"

"Yes! That's Mr. Fulton, right?"

"Um, no. That was Ethel's niece. Can you really not tell men and women apart?"

"I told you, all humans look the same. Can you tell whether a cat is a man or a woman just by glancing at them?"

Okay, he was right about that, so I decided to cut him a bit of slack.

He flicked his tail as he thought, then said, "I don't suppose you could describe what this Mr. Fulton smells like? It would be so much easier for me if you would."

"Um, no. Sorry." I shook my head to erase the mental image of me attempting to surreptitiously sniff my boss.

He shrugged and began grooming himself.

I slumped back against the couch again and sighed, something I sure was doing a lot of lately. "Then I guess nothing I tell you is of value because you don't even know who I'm talking about. How are we supposed to solve this thing if we can't even fully communicate with each other?"

It seemed like a cruel joke that I'd somehow

gained the ability to talk to animals but couldn't use that power to actually accomplish anything. Someone upstairs must be getting a good laugh out of the two of us right about now.

"You could take me to work with you," Octo-Cat chanced with a sly grin.

"No way. I already told you why that won't work." I still had no idea why he wanted to go to the office so badly, but this was one point on which I refused to waiver.

He looked bored as he suggested, "Okay, then how about the viewing tomorrow?"

I leapt up straight in my seat at this. "A viewing? Like the pre-funeral thing?"

"That was what I gathered. The humans were discussing it yesterday between the time you left and the time you came back." He meant when I'd gone to the hospital. It seemed no one was overly concerned about my near brush with death, not even my new friend, the talking cat. I tried not to let it hurt my feelings, but jeez. You'd think at least someone would be worried after a display like that.

"I don't know how," I told him, forcing myself to focus on the matter at hand once again. "But yes. I'm going to find a way to take you with me. Since the killer was someone Ethel knew well enough to have over for dinner, then he'll definitely be making an appearance. We need to be there, too."

"I was hoping you'd say that," he said with a wink. "Now, if you'll please excuse me, I need to pay a visit to the little kitty box."

CHAPTER TWELVE

I snuck out of work early the next day so that Octo-Cat and I could get ready for the viewing happening early that evening. Mr. Fulton didn't come into the office at all that day, which made it quite difficult for me to do any further investigation into his means or motive. The longer he stayed away, however, the more and more suspicious I became.

One way or another, I'd need to find a way to learn more. Maybe I could invite myself over to his house to visit with Diane. Or maybe the viewing would reveal everything I needed to know. I sure hoped it would be the latter.

Knowing that there was a killer on the loose—and that it was more than likely someone I personally knew—had started cutting into my sleep lately. Add Octo-Cat's early morning wakeup calls to the mix, and I was practically a dead woman walking. *Yikes.*

Until we had enough proof to take our case to the police, I'd just need to drink lots and lots of extra coffee, a pretty cruel irony considering how I'd first acquired my ability to talk to animals in the first place. I tried not to dwell on my near-death experience too much, considering that there was nothing *near* about Ethel Fulton's death.

On the way home I stopped off at the local charity shop to find a suitable mourning outfit. I also found an over-sized shoulder bag that I quickly claimed for that evening's use. Even though its tan and black wicker design appeared a tad on the beachy side, it would conceal Octo-Cat's furry bulk perfectly, thus allowing me to sneak him in and out of the funeral home undetected.

"It smells," he told me with a flick of his tail when I presented my idea to him a short while later.

Even though I knew the second-hand bag wouldn't be an easy sell for my spoiled cat friend, I still frowned with disappointment. "Unless you have a better idea, I'm afraid we're stuck."

"I was invited to the will reading. Why am I not

invited to this?" His upper lip quivered, and he let out a pitiful, weak mewling sound. It actually made me feel bad for him even though his ego could stand to be taken down a few pegs.

"Look, I didn't make the rules," I explained. "It's a public showing, which means pretty much anyone who wants to come is welcome, but I still worry they'll turn us both away if I show up with you out in the open. Sorry, it's just how most people would react to a cat showing up in a public place. Especially if you're still all freaked out from the car ride."

And now I'd made him angry. Well, angry was better than sad, I guess.

"You said I was getting better," he reminded me with a growl.

Okay, yes, I did tell him that on the way home from Ethel's estate a couple nights back, but it had only been a polite, little lie to make him feel better.

"Yes, that's right," I said now, unwilling to take the time to explain the intricacies of human etiquette to him when the clock was already ticking.

I left my feline friend to pout while I quickly changed into my new get-up. Sarcastic or not, Bethany had been absolutely right about Goodwill being a great place to find clothes within my budget. This new black dress fell just below my knees and could just as easily be repurposed for a cocktail party as it could a funeral.

"Let's go," I said, sweeping back through the living room and pointing to the wicker vehicle I'd purchased expressly for this mission.

Octo-Cat's eyes widened in horror. "Surely I don't need to get in there now. Can't it at least wait until we reach the funeral parlor?"

"Nope, I'm not taking any chances." I put one hand on my hip and used the other to hold the bag open wide. "Now in!"

He hissed and growled, but ultimately complied.

"Good kitty," I said.

Another hiss rose out of the bag. "I warned you about that."

"Yeah," I murmured as I twisted the lock on the front door after closing it behind me. "But you already puked on my bed once, so I figured I'd earned that one."

"You figured wrong," he said, popping his head out of the bag to scowl at me.

I laughed as I set his makeshift carrier on the floor of the passenger side, then off we went. Once or twice he tried to flee the bag for the safe harbor of my lap, but each time I managed to talk him off the ledge and back into his hiding place.

"I hate you so much," Octo-Cat snarled when at last we arrived.

"Shh," I warned him. "Nobody can know you're here."

Luckily the bag's weave gave him some visibility without revealing his hidden form. Just as much as I wanted to catch the killer, I also believed Octo-Cat deserved the chance to pay Ethel his respects. After all, she'd been an all-encompassing companion for him his entire life and I knew he missed her like crazy.

"Remember the plan," I murmured without moving my lips. Maybe all these years my hidden talent had actually lied in ventriloquism. I'd definitely have to explore it in more detail later.

"If you see—or, *umm*, smell—someone who was at the dinner party," I continued, "reach through the bag with your claws and tap my arm. Please note this is the only time I am giving you permission to claw me."

"Understood. Now please let's get this over with. This thing really stinks." He wasn't the only one who'd rather be at home, but it seemed I had to be strong now for the both of us.

I hoisted the bag further up my shoulder and strode forward with the confidence of someone who didn't have a talking cat secretly stashed in her bag. No sooner had we entered than I found a familiar, wrinkled visage staring right at me. Honestly, it gave me the heebie jeebies, especially after what Brad had revealed to me about her tantrum at the will reading.

"I recognize you," I said, striding straight up to her. "What's your name again?"

She glanced around then murmured, "Anne Fulton."

Octo-Cat chose that exact moment to sink his claws into the soft flesh beneath my arm.

"*Ow,*" I cried, then caught myself, chuckled nervously, and said, "'Ow did you know Ethel?"

"She was my aunt," Anne said, giving the answer I already knew.

"I'm sorry for your loss," I said, ducking my head and charging away. The last thing I needed was to be trapped with this strange, temperamental, breaking-and-entering woman all evening. Yet, then again, I was kind of all those things, too. Maybe Anne and I had more in common than I wanted to admit.

The bag weighed heavily on my shoulder,

making me think that maybe Octo-Cat would benefit from a diet and me from some more weight lifting. We passed gracelessly between the guests, making our way toward the casket.

There Ethel Fulton lay upon a bed of light pink silk, her short hairstyle curled in a perfect halo, her makeup heavy but elegant. I hadn't known her in life, but seeing her dead body laid on display like this sent a shiver of sorrow straight through me.

Octo-Cat clawed me a second time, and it stung. "Yes," I hissed quietly. "Ethel was at her own dinner party. I know that."

He let out a low growl then mumbled, "Incoming from behind."

I spun on my heel, resisting the urge to check my arm for little pin pricks of blood, and came face to face with Diane wearing a simple, black shift dress with an understated pillbox hat.

"Oh, Angie," she cried, falling into my arms so fast the bag almost slipped off my shoulder. "I'm so glad to see a friendly face."

She held tight to me for a long time, sobbing and sharing stories of all the good times she'd had with Ethel. "When I was a young bride, Ethel took me under her wing and taught me everything I needed to know to keep a good home and to keep my husband happy." Diane burst into another hysterical sob. "Oh, you don't have time for this."

"There, there," I said, patting her back and praying she would let me go.

She tensed in my arms and yanked away as if she'd been burned… or perhaps electrocuted.

I turned to see what she was staring at and saw Mr. Fulton standing in the entryway to the funeral home, with Bethany close at his side.

"I have to go," Diane sobbed, fleeing the scene before I had a chance to stop her.

Visions of the purple bra in Mr. Fulton's office danced before me menacingly. Now that I thought about it some more, that thing had looked like it was about Bethany's size. I watched in disgust as our boss placed his hand at the small of Bethany's back and guided her toward the casket, openly flaunting their intimacy for all to see.

Oh, poor Diane!

She had come to say goodbye to a beloved relative and instead her husband chose to humiliate her in front of the entire community.

I waited at the casket, wondering if they would even try to excuse their behavior. Octo-Cat slipped his claws through the bag's weave and dug those tiny pin missiles into me once more, alerting me to the fact that Mr. Fulton had, indeed, been present the night of the murder, too.

Well, now we knew the identity of three of the five guests from that night. Octo-Cat had already ruled out Anne for us, and I knew better than to suspect Diane. That narrowed our suspects to exactly three people. Either Mr. Fulton or one of the remaining mystery guests had done the deed—and more and more it looked like Fulton was our man.

"Angie," he said with a sad smile, dropping his hand from Bethany's back as he approached. "Thank you for coming to pay your respects."

Bethany nodded curtly but didn't say anything.

"It was the least I could do," I said, not knowing what I meant by that.

Apparently, however, my words were well received.

"She was such a special lady," Fulton said with a sigh. "Almost like a second mother. I've been having such a hard time admitting she's gone."

His voice cracked, and Bethany patted his arm consolingly. It only made me angrier and angrier.

They both turned to look into the casket, and I excused myself before I could say something we all regretted. Octo-Cat tapped me again as I charged through the other guests toward the door, but I didn't even notice who he wanted me to see.

At this point, I had all the proof I needed to know Mr. Fulton was guilty of at least two unforgivable crimes.

CHAPTER THIRTEEN

A hand on my shoulder stopped me before I could tear my way across the parking lot. I whipped around to see...

Bethany, of all people.

"What do you want?" I growled, not even bothering to disguise my disgust now.

Her wispy blonde hair rippled in the wind, and her lips pinched together in a tiny bow. I'd never seen her look this vulnerable—or this feminine—before. "I want to make sure you're okay. You looked like you were going to be sick back there. Have you never seen a dead body before?"

"I've seen bodies," I spat. "What I haven't seen is my boss flaunting his affair right in everyone's faces and at the very worst possible time, too."

Bethany gasped and took a step back. "Affair? You couldn't possibly think…"

"What else am I supposed to think?" I demanded, actually wishing she'd offer up another answer. I'd been quite happy working for Fulton, Thompson, and Associates until this recent turn of events. I'd never be able to look at Fulton or Bethany the same ever again, not without picturing that awful purple bra, his hand at her back and —*oh, yeah*—the murder of a sweet, old lady who definitely didn't deserve it.

Bethany frowned and shook her head. "I thought you knew me better than that by now, Angie." It almost looked like she might cry. Who was this frail woman before me, and why was she suddenly so different than the office shark who would sink her teeth into anyone to get ahead?

"I hardly know you at all. And I guess I don't know Mr. Fulton very well, either." I laughed bitterly. "You know, you guys did a great job hiding it. I actually had no idea until I came in early and found you two alone in the office. Then there was that bra—"

"A bra?" Bethany asked aloud, then mumbled something to herself that I couldn't quite make out.

Maybe now that she knew she'd been caught, she'd finally start telling me the truth here.

I crossed my arms, narrowing my gaze at her. "Yeah, *your* bra."

"Wow." She stared at me, unblinking. "Just wow."

"You honestly thought no one would ever find out? Just because I'm a paralegal doesn't make me any less intelligent than all you know-it-all lawyers." All my grievances were coming out now, all the things I'd kept to myself over the months in the name of creating a positive workplace environment. The way Bethany just stared at me with something that resembled hurt in her eyes was quite unsettling, though. I'd almost rather be dealing with Brad and his obnoxious come-ons right now.

Bethany kicked at the pavement in frustration. When her eyes snapped back up to mine, they were cold and unyielding. "Yes, and just because you're a woman doesn't mean you're not being terribly sexist right now, either. It's one thing for me to get this from the guys, but from you? I expected more of you, Angie."

"Oh, don't give me that whole 'I'm not angry, I'm disappointed' spiel. I heard it from my nan a million times growing up. And don't go placing the blame on me when you're the one sneaking around with a married man—who just so happens to also be our boss."

She widened her stance as if bracing for impact, then enunciated each word as she insisted, "I am not having an affair with Mr. Fulton."

"I don't know," I said with a shrug. "You two looked mighty cozy in there."

She glanced over her shoulder demurely. "That's different."

"Yeah, right." I smirked and gave her a sarcastic thumbs up. I wasn't normally such a confrontational person, but for some reason, Bethany just got under my skin, especially today at the viewing when emotions already ran high.

"It is," she insisted through gritted teeth. "You don't understand."

"Oh, I understand perfectly," I yelled. There was nothing I hated more than being condescended to—well, except maybe murder and adultery.

"No, you don't," she shouted back, then dropped her voice several notches. "And you're starting to make a scene."

What Bethany didn't understand is that I'd

never been bothered about making a scene. I was raised by a retired stage actress, for crying out loud! As far as we were concerned, making a scene was a good thing just so long as it didn't get us into trouble.

I could tell Bethany was getting ready to put an end to our exchange, so I finally decided to ask the million-dollar question. "Hey, you're the one who stopped me from leaving. But, okay, tell me this: if you're not having an affair, then what are the two of you doing?"

She wrapped both arms around her own waist and looked toward the ground as she murmured, "I can't tell you that. At least not yet."

"How convenient," I muttered while shaking my head.

When Bethany didn't say anything else, I charged the rest of the way across the lot and tossed my bag onto the passenger seat of my car, forgetting momentarily that Octo-Cat was stowed away inside. *Oops.*

"Do you mind?" he shouted after making the same terrible sound he most often uses to wake me up in the mornings. "Some of us are trying to avoid losing lives unnecessarily here."

Despite his irritation, he seemed to be okay.

But me? I was so angry that my hands shook and turned bright red. I needed a moment to re-center myself, but Octo-Cat did not like being ignored.

"Uh, hello, I'm talking here!" he shouted, taking a swipe at my arm with claws extended, which made me angrier still.

"Don't you ever shut up?" I yelled back at him.

"Wow, who pooped in your party?"

"That's not the expression," I said, still seething from the confrontation with Bethany. I just wanted to get home, but I didn't trust myself to drive safely yet.

My tabby nuisance put his two front paws on my leg and began to knead the muscle as he spoke. "It fits, though. Now you're the one who dragged me into this, you can at least include me. What was that back there?"

"*Me?* Dragging *you?* Yeah, that's not how I remember it."

"Semantics." He waved a paw dismissively and sat back down on his seat. "Who started this isn't what's important. What I want to know is why you got so hung up on a human that wasn't even there that night. Don't you care about finding Ethel's murderer?"

Suddenly, all the fight drained out of me as if Octo-Cat had twisted a spigot. No matter how scandalized I felt about the affair, Octo-Cat, no doubt, felt far worse. He'd lost someone important to him, and here I was making a circus out of her viewing.

"I'm sorry," I murmured, feeling like the worst friend in the world.

"Hey, it's okay. Humans get emotional sometimes." He licked at his paw idly, then added, "Okay, a lot of times. But we can work through this."

His words were oddly comforting and just what I needed.

"Okay," I said, letting out a slow, shaky breath. "Okay."

Octo-Cat nodded. "We need to go back in," he informed me. "We still haven't found everyone who was there that night."

"I think I already know who killed Ethel," I confessed. "All signs point to Mr. Fulton."

"The man. My boss," I clarified when I noticed he still looked confused.

As it turned out, what my kitty companion said next shocked me with its wisdom and depth.

"Look," he said. "He could very well be the one, but we can't know for sure until we rule the others out. It's like how sometimes you might think that the chicken pâté is your favorite flavor of Fancy Feast, but then the next day you have the salmon and shrimp blend and it tastes even better than the chicken. When you think about it some more, you may have just been extra hungry before which made the inferior flavor of the chicken seem extra delicious, or you mistakenly thought chicken was best only because you hadn't tried all the other wonderful flavors yet. Do you get what I'm saying?"

Strangely, I did. "That Mr. Fulton could be our salmon and shrimp blend, or he could simply be chicken pâté, but we won't know until we've finished our meal?"

"Exactly." He seemed to glow with pride, but maybe that was just his eyes glinting in the waning sunlight. "This meal's only just getting started, so make sure you save some space in that belly of yours."

"Thanks, Octo-Cat. I needed that."

"And I may need you to swing by the store after this and grab some chicken pâté. I know, I know. I usually don't eat the poultry flavors, but suddenly I find myself with a craving."

I scratched him between the ears. "You're a good cat."

"And you're a very good human. Yes, you are," he told me in a goochie-goo voice that made us both smile. "Now let's get back inside and see who else we can find."

CHAPTER FOURTEEN

E ven though Octo-Cat convinced me to go back into the funeral home for the viewing, we were too late to do any meaningful sleuthing. The close family and friends had already departed for a private function, leaving only distant acquaintances and curious casket-gawkers to mingle in the parlor.

Unsurprisingly, Bethany had left, too, only further supporting my suspicions.

Octo-Cat and I were among the last to remain behind, which gave him a chance to surreptitiously poke his head out of the bag and speak his good-byes to Ethel.

"Oh, Ethel," he cried without a trace of his normal over-the-top theatrics. "You were my whole world, and you didn't even know it. I know we had our disagreements on occasion, but you were truly the best thing that ever happened to me. The world won't be quite as bright without you in it. I'll always think of you when drinking Evian or stretching out in a sun spot. I love you and am so happy you were my human."

I teared up a bit as I listened to his heartfelt goodbye. "That was beautiful," I told him, searching around for one of the boxes of tissues I'd spotted earlier, but coming up short.

"Yeah," he said with a sniff and a twitch of his whiskers.

"By the way," I said, settling him back into the bag with the utmost care. "She knew how important she was to you."

His voice came out muffled. "How can you be sure?"

"I just am."

After that, we drove home, and I briefly stopped off at the supermarket to purchase fresh shrimp for our dinner. Octo-Cat had kept it together when I couldn't. As far as I was concerned, he'd more than earned this special treat. Seeing as it would be impossible for me to prepare such a nice meal without also indulging, I bought enough to feed me, too.

Octo-Cat didn't eat as much as he normally did, which worried me. "Is your dinner okay?" I asked regarding the morsel on my fork suspiciously. Could he sense something I didn't? My mind briefly flitted back to smelling dishes in Ethel's kitchen in an ill-fated attempt to detect poison.

He sighed. "I just miss Ethel."

"Of course, you do. I'm so sorry you had to see her like that."

"It's just…" He sniffed as he padded his paws on the table anxiously. "It's just, I thought we'd be together forever. Then suddenly she was gone."

"Life works like that sometimes," I admitted, never having felt this acute sense of loss myself but hoping I could still offer some measure of comfort.

"If you want, maybe…" I hesitated, something new and most definitely unexpected overtaking me.

"Yeah?" he asked sadly, when I didn't continue.

"Maybe after this is all said and done, I don't know…"

Just say it!

"Well, maybe I could be your human."

His eyes widened with surprise, and then a

rumbling purr filled the silence between us. "I'd like that," he said.

"I mean, it's better than having to break in another new human." He dropped his head and nibbled on the largest and most succulent shrimp I had placed before him.

Now that he was otherwise occupied, he was unable to see the tears welling in the corners of my eyes.

What could I say?

That ornery tabby had really grown on me the past few days. Maybe I was a cat person after all.

The next morning, I woke up before Octo-Cat could rouse me—and unbelievably I felt refreshed and ready to go. Excited for the day ahead, even. It was such a drastic change from how I'd felt upon going to bed that it couldn't have been anything other than a gift from above.

Rather than questioning it, I decided to pay it forward.

"I have a present for you," I told Octo-Cat after he'd finished his breakfast.

"Not another foul-smelling bag, I hope," he

complained, but I could tell he was excited. Something about the twitch of his tail and the perkiness with which he trailed me back toward the bedroom suggested he was in just as good a mood as me that day. Perhaps how we'd bonded over our shrimp dinner last night had something to do with it.

"Hop up," I told him as I took a seat on the bed and rooted around in my night stand.

He joined me, padding across my lap to sniff at the drawer.

When I pulled out what I was looking for, he leapt back with a start. "What's that thing?" he said between quick, panicked breaths.

"This is my iPad," I explained, pushing the power button to wake the screen then setting it on the bed between us. "Well, actually now it's yours."

"It's shiny," he commented, sniffing it hesitantly.

I nodded enthusiastically. "Yes, and I think you'll really like what it can do."

"Oh?" Now I had his interest.

"I'm guessing Ethel didn't have one of these," I said, presenting it once again with a flourish.

He shook his head in confirmation.

"Well, we can install apps for you to play with when you're bored, like a virtual fish tank or a keyboard or even the radio, and we will… But the main reason I'm giving this to you is for FaceTime."

"FaceTime?" He laughed after trying the name aloud for himself. "That's an odd mash up of unrelated words."

"Yeah, but they already had iPhone, so they had to come up with something else to name this app. Look." I pulled my phone out of my pocket and called the tablet using FaceTime.

Oct-Cat swished his tail as he watched me reach over to answer the call. "Whoa," he murmured in awe when my face popped up on the screen, followed by his own when I pointed the phone on my camera toward him.

"Cool, right?" I gushed. I loved teaching others new things just as much as I loved learning them for myself.

"What else can it do?" he asked, spinning in an excited circle before settling back down before the iPad.

"I know you miss me while I'm at work, so I figured we could use this system to talk to each other," I explained with an ingratiating smile, just in case he planned to argue this point. I was pleasantly surprised when he didn't.

My iPad was part of Nan's family network,

while my phone was funded by Fulton, Thompson, and Associates, which thankfully meant I had two separate numbers. Earlier, I'd found that to be a pain, but it worked out quite well now that my talking cat needed his own line.

I sat with him for about half an hour, teaching him how to unlock the device, click on the Face-Time app, and press my photo to call me. We also practiced having me call him, so he could answer by stepping on the screen with his paw.

And he did it all splendidly.

Who said cats couldn't be trained?

By the time I had to leave for work, Octo-Cat was pleasantly pre-occupied with a koi fish app he'd selected all on his own. He didn't play the game quite right, but he sure had fun swiping at the fish on screen.

So, I left him to it and headed to the firm to see what more I could learn that day.

As it turned out, it wasn't much. Mr. Thompson had taken Derek to court with him. Bethany refused to speak so much as a word to me, and I generally preferred to avoid Brad as a rule. That left a few of our less talkative associates, Mr. Fulton, and me.

For his part, my boss seemed far more composed today than he had earlier in the week. I wondered if he'd made up with Diane. I also wondered if Bethany had told him about our heated exchange last night in the parking lot, but if she had, he showed no signs of knowing I suspected him of anything unsavory, affair or otherwise.

He approached my desk and cleared his throat. "Angie," he said, his mouth set in a firm line. "I need you to work on a special project for me today."

I looked up from my keyboard and nodded. "Sure. What can I do for you?"

He rapped his fingers on the edge of my desk, and we both watched his hand as he spoke.

"I need you to search for some precedents about wills being thrown out due to the guarantors being of unsound mind at the time of signing. What were their arguments? What happened to the estate after the original will was discarded? How long did the cases take to settle?"

He paused, slipped both hands in his pockets, and glanced over his shoulder before continuing.

"But before that, could you, um, do a quick review of a petition for me and then send it through the courier? I'd really like it to go out today, please."

"Yes, absolutely," I answered without hesitation.

He broke out into a huge smile. "Great. That'll

be a huge help. I'll email the petition shortly." He turned and walked back to his office with a somewhat lighter gait than he'd used to approach.

It hardly took a minute for the document to pop up in my inbox. Curious, I clicked to download the attachment.

It was a petition for divorce.

His divorce from Diane.

CHAPTER FIFTEEN

After a quick scan of the divorce petition, I snuck into the bathroom at work to call Octo-Cat. It took two tries before he answered, and when he did, I couldn't see anything on the screen.

"Hello?" I asked, unsure about the stability of our connection.

"Hello," he answered, his voice coming over loud and clear and full of pride. "I did it!"

I stared at the screen, still unable to make out his picture. "Why can't I see you?"

"I don't know," came his befuddled response. "I mean, I'm sitting right on the thing!"

Well, that explained a lot. I'd have to gently remind him how the camera works later that night. For now, I was far too excited about the new information I had to share and preferred not to spoil it by getting in to a lengthy argument over proper iPad usage for cats.

I dropped my voice to a whisper to make sure no one else in the building could hear me. "Mr. Fulton is filing for a divorce. He also has me researching a bunch of old cases related to over-turning wills. I think he might be our shrimp and salmon blend after all."

"What does that mean?" Octo-Cat asked without the slightest hint of irony in his voice. Could he have really forgotten his own metaphor?

"Yesterday, you… *Never mind.*" I couldn't get into this with him, not when we had far more important matters to discuss. Not when I already had a massive headache forming at the edges of my brain.

"Just tell me this," I said, determined to make something of this call. "What do you think it all means?"

Octo-Cat let out a loud and long yawn. "You're right that it makes him seem guilty. Mr. Fulton, *hmm…* Which one is he again?"

I sighed and clutched my forehead in my hands. We were quickly heading to migraine status. "I'll point him out at the funeral, okay?" I offered with a whimper.

"Sure." He yawned again. "When is that again?"

I was seriously beginning to worry here. It's like my cat's entire mind had been wiped clean overnight. "Hey, *um*, are you okay?"

"I just woke up from a nap, so I'm a little out of sorts," he admitted with another high-pitched yawn. "And the longer we talk, the warmer this thing is getting. It's making me so sleepy."

That's what happens when you sit on your iPad, I thought. "Okay, well, I'll let you go then. Enjoy your nap."

"Oh, I shall," he said right before I ended the call.

Well, that had accomplished nothing, other than telling me that FaceTime could possibly work as a method of communication for us with a bit more practice on Octo-Cat's end.

I washed my hands and then stepped out of the bathroom, back into the main office.

Mr. Fulton was waiting just outside the door. "Did you finish that petition for me yet?" he asked anxiously.

"Just about," I promised.

"Good." He nodded, but continued to frown. "I need that research ASAP, too."

"You've got it." He looked like he wanted to say something more, so I stood awkwardly by and waited for him to gather his thoughts.

Mr. Fulton frowned as he regarded me, which I tried not to take personally. Even though I was trying to prove him guilty of murder, I was still great at my job as a paralegal.

"I'll be headed out of the office soon and plan on taking tomorrow and Monday for personal affairs," he informed me with a dismissive nod.

Affairs. I practically choked at his choices of words but managed to hold it together well enough to say, "Okay, I'll put everything else on hold until I get that done for you."

Finally, he switched his expression to something less aggrieved and a bit more neutral. It still wasn't quite a smile, but I'd take it. "Good. Thank you, Angie. See you next week."

I watched him return to his office, then shut and lock the door. What could he possibly be hiding in there? And where was he headed for the long weekend?

I briefly debated calling Octo-Cat again, but the poor furball clearly needed his rest. Still, I needed someone to talk to, so I took a big gamble and headed to Bethany's office, hoping enough time had passed that she'd at least be willing to talk with me.

I knocked softly at her door, wishing I had some kind of peace offering. For now, my apology would have to do.

"Go away, please," she called without opening the door.

"I'm sorry about yesterday," I pleaded into the cherry-stained wood. "I was hoping we could talk about it."

The door flung open to reveal my still very clearly enraged coworker. "What's there to talk about?" she demanded with a hand on her hip and a scowl on her face.

"I'm just worried about you and wanted to see if you needed to talk." This much was true. If she was carousing with a murderer, she definitely needed to know that. As much as Bethany got on my nerves sometimes, I'd much rather have her on my team than playing against me.

"No thanks," she answered, trying to close the door again.

I stuck my foot into the door's path just in time. "Please, just give me two minutes," I begged.

"Fine." She retreated back to the safety of her desk and stared daggers at me.

I closed the door behind me and slowly approached.

"Time's a ticking," she reminded me, pointing at her wrist even though she'd never worn a watch as long as I'd known her.

"Look, I don't know what's going on with you and Mr. Fulton, but I'm worried about you," I started.

She let out a sigh so big, it ruffled some of the papers on her desk. "Not this again."

"Bethany, listen to me. I have reason to believe he's dangerous."

She shook her head. "That's ridiculous. Mr. Fulton is one of the most legitimately kind people I know."

"He's leaving the office for several days," I blurted out. It was definitely unusual behavior. Normally, he worked straight through the weekends, and I wanted to know what had changed about this week. "Do you know why?"

"I don't know… Maybe mourning? Why can't you just leave the poor man alone? And leave me alone, too, for that matter. Time's up, by the way."

"What? But we hardly even said anything at all," I protested.

"This is my office," she said as she rose from her

seat and marched toward the door. "I decide who is and isn't welcome. And right now, you most definitely aren't."

Defeated, I trailed after her. "Just be careful, okay?" I said once I'd made it into the hall.

"Sure, whatever," she said with a grimace, hesitating with her hand on the door knob. She hadn't closed me out, not yet.

Bethany bit her lip and studied me for a moment before suggesting, "I think you should talk to Brad about that bra you mentioned yesterday. I overheard him bragging to Derek about some after-hours conquest, and well... I'm sure he'll be more than happy to tell you the rest."

She shut the door in my face—a bit gentler this time, so at least we were making progress. Opting to take her advice, I headed to Brad's office next.

I hated that we didn't have Derek as a buffer today. He was usually the only one who could keep Brad even close to in control. Still, I needed answers, and I needed them much sooner than later.

"What's up, doll face?" he asked when I clicked his door shut behind me.

"Doll face? Really?" I shuddered. First of all,

that pet term was from at least eight decades ago, and second, it wasn't at all appropriate for work.

"What? You prefer sweet cheeks?" He glanced pointedly toward my rear and widened his eyes in what I assumed was appreciation. *Gross.*

"What I want is for you to call me my name and only my name," I ground out, taking great care not to slap him across the face—at least not before getting the info I'd come for. "It's Angie, by the way," I reminded him.

"Okay, Angie," he said pointedly, smirking up at me. "What can I do you for?"

I decided to just spit it out so that I could spend as little time alone with this walking lawsuit as possible. "What do you know about the purple silk bra I found in Mr. Fulton's office yesterday?"

His smile widened to a sickening degree. "Heard about that, did you?"

"I *saw* it," I said, shuddering again.

He chuckled. "Aww, don't be jealous. There's plenty of Brad to go around."

"So, it *was* yours," I spat.

"Not mine, but…" He shot me a creepy smile as he thought of how to put it. "A friend's," he finally settled on.

"If it was your friend's, then what was it doing in Mr. Fulton's office?" I demanded.

He shrugged casually. "My friend may have thought I was the junior partner here."

"And why would she think that?"

He sighed and shook his head. "C'mon, Angie. Do I really need to spell it out for you?"

Ick, ick, ick. "Does Mr. Fulton know?"

He cleared his throat. "Of course not. You think I want to be put on suspension?"

"No, but you deserve it. Worse, even," I hissed, giving him one last withering look before charging out of his office.

Finally, the firm had enough reason to send Brad packing. I didn't care how influential and well respected his father was. Brad was, hands down, the biggest creep I'd ever met. He should have been fired months ago for sexual harassment, but then again, it was possible that neither Thompson nor Fulton knew since Bethany and I tended to let his disgusting behavior carry on unchecked.

Well, no more.

I barged straight to Fulton's office, forgetting to knock.

I found him on the phone, speaking in a raspy

whisper. "I don't care what it takes," he growled. "Keep it buried. At least until the divorce is final."

Our eyes locked, and his face contorted in momentary rage before he wiped his expression clean once again. I should have turned on my heel and run away but was too startled to move a muscle. Stupid deer in headlights effect.

"I'll talk to you later," he whispered into the phone, then turned his full attention to me and plastered on the most inauthentic smile I'd ever seen in all my life. "Angie, do you have my petition ready?"

"Yeah, let me just go get it," I lied, then I booked it out of there as fast as my legs could carry me.

Brad's dismissal would have to wait for another day. Right now, I had to make sure that I wasn't next on the chopping block. I'd happily give up my job, however, if it meant keeping my head.

CHAPTER SIXTEEN

Luckily, Mr. Fulton left shortly after I summoned the courier, which meant I was safe for the time being. I'd definitely be looking over my shoulder extra until he was behind bars, though.

When I told Octo-Cat about the call I'd overhead, even he had to agree that no one but Mr. Fulton could be to blame for Ethel's murder.

"And if he's killed before, it'll be easier for him to do it again," he added.

I shivered in fear. "You're right, and I'm pretty sure he knows that *I* know."

"Based on what you've told me, you're probably right." Octo-Cat rubbed his head against my arm affectionately, but it wasn't enough to put my mind at ease. Suddenly, every lingering shadow, every unexpected sound transformed into a warning that my boss was coming to kill me for what basically amounted to being too good at my job. Then again, I was supposed to be researching legal precedents, not clues in a murder mystery.

"We need to get out of here," I said, panic rising in my chest.

Octo-Cat looked up at me with large, amber eyes and an understanding nod. "Where to? Ethel's house?"

"Heck no!" I practically shouted. "We're going to Nan's."

I packed up his Fancy Feast, Evian, and freshly cleaned litter box in a hurry, feeling far too exposed in my own home.

"Don't forget my iPad," he reminded me as he pawed at the bedroom door. He seemed far less frightened than I did. Was this because he had nine lives to draw on? Whatever the case, he hadn't seen the livid expression on Mr. Fulton's face when he caught me eavesdropping on his call. If looks could kill...

No, if I focused too much on my fear, I wouldn't be able to act to keep myself safe. Right now, I just needed to focus on getting us out of there. Once we were out of there, we could brainstorm the best way to present our case to local law enforcement. Maybe Nan would have some good ideas about how to repackage our evidence in such a way that excluded the fact our primary informant was a talking cat.

Less than fifteen minutes later, Octo-Cat and I turned up at Nan's door with our overnight bags. Thank goodness for small towns and short drives.

"Angie?" my grandmother asked, blinking first at me and then at the tabby who stood at my side.

"What a nice surprise," she exclaimed, motioning us in and saddling me with a huge hug. She didn't even ask about the cat I'd randomly acquired since our last meeting. It all made me feel very guilty and like I should probably visit my nan more often.

She led us to the couch, and Octo-Cat immediately hopped up on her lap and began to purr.

"I like her," he announced. "She reminds me of Ethel."

"He likes you," I told her.

"I like him, too," she cooed. "Is he yours?" Today she wore an emerald green blouse with gemstones hand-sewn around the neck, and it suited her perfectly. I glanced down at the jeans and T-shirt I'd changed into after work, suddenly feeling underdressed for our visit. Then again, I was always coming up short compared to my elegant and talented Nan.

I shook my head and frowned. *"No.* Well, maybe. It's kind of a long story."

"I have time. Tell me what's going on." She continued to pet Octo-Cat while she listened to my tale of unexpected workplace terror.

Once I started talking, I just couldn't stop. It felt so nice to be able to unload it all on someone I knew was actually paying attention for a change. I caught her up on all the evidence against Mr. Fulton and what were more than likely false accusations toward Bethany. Now that I thought about it, I definitely owed her an apology. A sincere and heartfelt one.

"It sounds like something straight out of an off-Broadway script," Nan said, summing things up pretty accurately. "One thing I don't quite understand, though, is how you suspected murder in the first place."

I glanced toward Octo-Cat for guidance.

"You might as well tell her," he said, leaving Nan to take up residence on my lap. "You can pet me, if it helps," he offered selflessly.

"Thank you," I mumbled.

"Thank you for what, dear?" Nan asked with an unassuming smile.

Why was I holding back? If I couldn't trust Nan —the very woman who had raised me—then I had no hope left for this life, anyway. Besides, it would be nice to finally share my secret with someone outside of Octo-Cat.

I took a deep breath, pushing my fingers through his fur as I prepared for my big reveal. "Remember how you picked me up from the hospital earlier this week?" Man, could it really only be Thursday with all that had happened these past few days? My entire world had changed in the blink of a cat's eye.

Nan nodded. "You said it was a mild electric shock. Was it something more than that?" she pressed, reaching for her bifocals so she could study my face more closely as we talked.

"It was an electrical shock, that part's totally true. What I didn't tell you, though…" I bit my lip. What would I do if Nan didn't believe me?

"Go on," Octo-Cat encouraged me. "She can handle it."

"Go on," Nan also said. Her wrinkled brow knitted with worry while she waited. As much as my forthcoming confession unnerved me, I couldn't leave her hanging like that.

"I can talk to cats," I blurted out, finally putting it out there for the wider universe's consideration.

She glanced from me to Octo-Cat and back again. "Does he talk?" she asked considering my big reveal for a few seconds.

"Yes, he does," I nodded enthusiastically. Did this mean she actually believed me? "He's the one who told me about Ethel's murder. She was his owner, and he saw the whole thing," I further explained.

"I'm so sorry your owner was murdered like that," she told Octo-Cat, patting her lap and inviting him to return to her. "Is there anything I can do to help?"

And this right here was one of the many reasons I loved my nan so dearly. She didn't question my crazy claim. She just automatically believed what I told her. We all need someone like Nan in our corner.

Relief washed over me as I realized I'd done the right thing by trusting her with my secret. "Did you understand her?" I asked Octo-Cat.

"Yes, I did," he informed me, then looked up at Nan and said, "Thank you for your condolences."

"Oh," Nan cried. "He's talking to me! What did that adorable, little meow mean?"

Octo-Cat beamed with pure and unadulterated joy. Apparently, it was okay for Nan to dote on him in a way that I wasn't quite allowed yet.

"He thanked you for your condolences," I passed on.

"What a well-mannered fella you are," she said, stroking him up and down his back. Octo-Cat now seemed to live on cloud nine, and I didn't want to ruin the moment for either of them by reminding everyone of just how rude my cat companion was on the regular.

"I'm worried, Nan," I confessed. "I'm almost positive Mr. Fulton poisoned his aunt, but the police probably won't believe the whole talking cat informant angle as readily as you did."

"Good point," she said with a defeated frown.

"So where does that leave us?" I begged for an answer. "I can't exactly live the rest of my life on edge until he's caught, but I also can't go to the police with this. Even if I were to quit my job and move back in with you, that still wouldn't guarantee anyone's safety. And it wouldn't avenge Ethel, either. Besides, what if Mr. Fulton is planning to strike again?"

Nan and I both thought on this in relative silence as Octo-Cat purred his content at receiving Nan's idle attentions. I meditated on my last question. Even if Mr. Fulton did kill again, would I really be the most likely candidate? It made far more sense that...

"Oh my gosh, Diane!" I shouted with this sudden realization. "She doesn't know!"

Of course! Add the fact that Mr. Fulton had said he wanted to keep his dirty secret until after the divorce was finalized to the other simple fact he was filing for divorce in the first place, and it clearly painted Diane Fulton as the one who was most in danger should he decide to strike again.

The divorce itself already showed he had no love left for the soon-to-be-former Mrs. Fulton. What if she pushed him too hard during the divorce proceedings? What if she was next? She didn't have any idea she could be in danger...

I popped to my feet, suddenly desperate to get to my friend and make sure she was okay.

"Now just you hold on, missy," Nan said, pulling herself to her feet and placing a hand on my shoulder. "You came here because you were afraid for your safety. I'm not letting you rush off straight into the lion's den. Regardless of the source, you have a pretty solid case against Mr. Fulton—and it sounds like he might know it, too. The last thing you want to do now is to turn up at his house with these accusations of yours."

Our eyes met, hers pleading while mine stared ahead unblinking. This was my nan, the one person who loved me more than anything in the whole wide world. Of course, she only wanted what was best for me. But at the end of the day, I couldn't stand by if it meant possibly signing my friend's death warrant.

I ripped my arm away from Nan. "I'm sorry, but I don't have any choice," I shouted, already on my way out the door.

CHAPTER SEVENTEEN

I was surprised when Nan didn't try to stop me. Far less surprising, though, was the fact that Octo-Cat seemed to think he was coming with me. A brown blur shot past me as I ran toward my car.

"Let's do this," the tabby said with a look of determination I would have found comical if not for the seriousness of the situation.

"You're not coming," I shouted. I didn't have time for this. What if I was too late to warn Diane? "Now get out of my way."

He kept his focus glued firmly on my car door, waiting for me to open it. "Oh, I see. I'm only allowed to come when *you* think you need me."

"That's right," I grumped. "And I don't need

you for this. Go stay with Nan and wait for me to come back."

His tail flicked wildly back and forth as he regarded me with hurt reflecting in his eyes. "You're really mean sometimes. You know that?"

"And you're really annoying all the time," I yelled back while silently begging for him to give up the fight. The last thing I needed was for him to be in danger, too. Despite my better judgment, I'd really come to love the little nuisance.

"Whatever," he said with a growl, staring me down. When at last I opened the car door, he hopped right in despite my consistent objections.

So, I did the worst possible thing I could think of. I picked him up by the scruff of his neck and marched him straight back to the house.

"Let go of me," Octo-Cat cried as he twisted violently in a futile attempt to escape my grip. "This is not okay!"

Without saying anything more, I tossed him into the house and slammed the door shut before he could regain his bearings. As much as I'd miss my sassy sidekick, it was better this way. Besides, if I brought him with me, Diane might suggest I leave him with her. I couldn't stand the thought of losing my new friend—but I also knew I wouldn't be strong enough to refuse if she asked.

I still didn't know how to convince the extended, non-murdering side of the Fulton family to let me keep him, but I'd have time to figure that out later. Right now, I had to save Diane from meeting a fate similar to Ethel's.

Although we probably wouldn't see each other much anymore, considering the divorce and the likelihood of her ex eventually ending up in jail, I still cared about her and wanted her to be all right. At the end of the day, I wouldn't wish death on anyone, not even Brad and especially not poor Diane who had been through so much already.

I owed her at least this much in honor of the brief, reality-TV based friendship we'd shared these past few months.

I'd only been to the Fulton's home once before to attend a company potluck over the holidays, but I still remembered the exact location of their fancy McMansion. After all, Blueberry Bay wasn't that big of a region, and our town of Glendale was even tinier.

I pulled up outside the white vinyl facade, which was offset by a massive front lawn, and cut my engine. Perhaps a call to announce my arrival would have been in order, but I didn't want to risk Mr. Fulton finding out I was headed here before I at least had a chance to warn Diane about the dangers that lurked right in her very own broken home.

Marching right up to the front door with far more confidence than I felt, I tried the handle without first ringing the doorbell to announce myself. Of course, since this was small-town Maine, the door stood unlocked. I let myself in, hoping that I wasn't too late to make a difference.

Inside, the house was dark as dusk settled over the land.

"Hello? Diane?" I called, groping about for a light switch but coming up short.

I padded toward the living room but turned abruptly when I heard the sound of a floorboard creak from a few paces behind me. There, within the pale light of the large bay window, a tall shadowy figure stood with its arms stretched high overhead.

"Diane?" I asked, squinting at the figure and praying it was my friend rather than her husband. I didn't have long to puzzle it out, though, because…

CRACK!

A tremendous pain radiated from my forehead, and before I had the chance to figure out what was going on, I crumpled to the floor, having once again lost consciousness.

When I came to, every inch of my body screamed with pain. I looked to my left and saw a massive fire roaring in the fireplace less than a foot away. It was too close. My skin had already begun to turn red from the excessive warmth. Struggling to move out of its range, I realized then that both my hands and my feet had been bound together in front of me.

"You think you can just break into somebody's home?" my captor rasped, moving into the light. I fully expected to see Mr. Fulton standing before me, but no. It wasn't him at all.

It was Diane, my friend. *My attacker? What?*

"Diane," I wheezed. "It's me, Angie. We need to get out of here."

"I know who you are. What I don't know is why you couldn't leave well enough alone." The contempt that filled her eyes as they combed over me was so blatant that I could hardly recognize the kindly woman I'd come to consider a friend.

My head pulsed with pain, making it hard to

think straight. Why was she acting like this? Had Mr. Fulton lied to her about everything? Did she somehow think I was to blame for all of this?

None of this was adding up.

"Ethel was murdered!" I screamed at her. My throat ached just like the rest of me, but I didn't care. "We have to tell someone."

Diane groaned and paced the room in search of something. "Keep quiet," she warned. Maybe this was all an act. Maybe she was scared, too, and trying to convince Mr. Fulton she was on his side so that he wouldn't harm her.

"Let me go," I pleaded. "It's not too late. We can go to the police, and—"

She rushed back toward me and stooped down so we were at eye level. "Nobody's going to the police," she said in an eerie whisper before slapping me right across my face.

As this new pain stung my cheek, I finally saw the truth that stood right before me. Mr. Fulton had never been guilty—not of murder, not of this.

"It was you the whole time," I spat.

She smiled a wicked grin and rolled her eyes. *"Obviously.* Don't act like you didn't know. I couldn't believe my dumb luck when you woke up at the will reading talking about a murder. I've heard about psychics before, but I had no idea you were one of them."

"You think I'm a psychic?" I hissed. Everything hurt, but most of all my heart. I'd been so naïve, blindly trusting Diane because we liked the same TV shows. Now this oversight could very well cost me my life.

"How else would you explain your inexplicable knowledge of Ethel's murder? At first, I thought maybe you were playing some kind of joke and had just accidentally blurted out something true without even knowing it, but then you kept turning up everywhere."

I shook my head and struggled against my bonds to no avail. It made sense that Diane thought I had psychic powers. In a way I did, just not in the way she'd assumed.

"The viewing, Ethel's house…" Diane continued, kicking me back when she saw that I was trying to untie my feet.

"Oh, don't look so shocked. Of course, Anne told me about that. The one thing I couldn't piece together is why you hadn't gone to the police to turn me in. But then when you tried to break into my house, I realized you actually planned to take me out yourself. Well, great job, you did." She laughed an evil villain laugh that seemed so at odds with the sweater-set-wearing, pearl clutching house-wife I knew.

"But *why?* Why would you kill Ethel?" I choked out. As much as I wanted to hear the answer, I needed to keep her talking until I could figure out a way to escape. For all I knew, she planned to kill me after our little talk here. Clearly this madwoman was capable of anything.

Diane snarled like a wild animal, baring her teeth and sending another chill straight to my gut. "Didn't you figure that part out when you helped my philandering oaf of a husband serve me with a petition for divorce today?"

I gasped, a response she clearly appreciated.

"So, he *was* sleeping with Bethany!" I said, playing it up to keep her talking as long as possible. I'd been wrong about our killer, but right about the affair. Whether or not the bra belonged to Bethany, she was still guilty.

"Sleeping with her?" Diane curled her nose in disgust and pushed off the floor back to a standing position.

My phone vibrated in my hip pocket, which gave me an idea. If I could just find a way to Face-Time Octo-Cat, he could get Nan and she could get the police. I needed to distract Diane enough that she wouldn't see me reaching into my pocket. It would be hard to be sly with my hands bound together, but I at least had to try.

"So he wasn't?" I asked curiously.

"I should hope not, seeing as she's his daughter. Then again, Richard's illegitimate child is the least of my problems right now." She moved fast, muttering to herself on occasion before speaking more to me.

How had she hidden so much of her true self? How had I never seen through the pleasant house-wife act? Did Mr. Fulton know? Is that why he was leaving her? I wanted to know so much more, but first, I needed to get away from the crazy murderess who now paced the floor in front of me.

"And you wanted all of Ethel's money for your-self," I said, hoping it was enough of a prompt to get her to fly into another monologue about her motives.

"Who wouldn't want the money? It's not like the old lady was long for this world anyway. I gave her an easy death which, if you ask me, was far better than she deserved."

As she talked, I inched my hands closer to my pocket. Luckily, my phone was on the opposite side of the fire, which gave me some shadows to help disguise my movements.

"You're already rich," I murmured, happy she wasn't looking at me anymore.

Diane had now returned to her frantic search of the room. I prayed it wasn't a gun she was hoping to find. I may be able to think fast, but I didn't think I'd be able to act fast enough to dodge a speeding bullet aimed straight at me, especially considering my recent head injury.

She laughed bitterly. "Already rich as Mrs. Fulton. What do you think will happen to me after the divorce, though?" Luckily, this was a rhetorical question as she kept talking without waiting to see what I had to say. "I thought I had more time. Richard was supposed to inherit everything from his aunt, then I'd get half if I could just keep him happy long enough for the will to go through. I got sick of waiting for the old lady to kick the bucket, so I helped her along. I couldn't believe my rotten luck when we found out she'd recently changed her will to leave almost everything to that stupid cat!"

I kept my eyes glued to Diane as I slipped the tips of my fingers into my pocket and began to slip the phone out from inside. She continued on her diatribe about her poor, unfair life, but I only heard enough to offer the smallest of replies. Instead, my focus had shifted toward my phone.

I pressed to unlock it—thankful I'd disabled the passcode—clicked the FaceTime app icon, and placed a call to Octo-Cat on my iPad.

Fingers crossed he wasn't too mad to help save my life.

CHAPTER EIGHTEEN

The call went through, and Octo-Cat answered after just a couple rings. I swear I'd never been happier to hear anyone's voice in all my life.

"Let me guess," he said, sounding almost bored. "You're in danger and need the cat to come save the day."

Yes! I wanted to scream, but I couldn't alert Diane to the call without causing serious trouble for myself. Instead, I needed to find a way to keep her talking until my cat could come up with a way to rescue me. Seriously, of all the things my life could hinge on, it all came down to a talking cat with a bad attitude—one whom I'd recently made very, very angry with me.

I needed to find a way to keep the conversation going, but Diane wasn't paying any attention to me as she ripped through drawers and containers in search of whatever it was she needed. A couple minutes later she found what she'd been searching for all this time and strode back across the room to show me. Oh, how I prayed Octo-Cat was still with me!

I pushed the phone behind my back by making a big show of struggling against my bonds, managing to get it out of sight just in time.

"I'd stop that if I were you," Diane warned, holding up the newly acquired object so that I could see it clearly. An old revolver caught and reflected the light of the fire in its smooth metal body, and no matter how much it terrified me, I just couldn't tear my eyes away.

"That's right," my captor said with a smirk. "You're going to die."

My mind reeled, turning back to Octo-Cat once more. I couldn't hear his voice anymore. For all I knew, we'd lost the connection or he'd gotten bored and given up waiting. Still, I had to press on with my plan, hoping he was there and listening with Nan.

"I can keep quiet," I pleaded with Diane. "I

don't have to tell anyone you murdered Ethel. You can take the money and leave. Or I can leave. Please. Just let me go."

"Oh, Angie," she said with false pity. "You're forgetting that I know you. You can't even keep the results of a TV singing competition secret. What makes you think I'd trust you with something like this?"

"Are you going to shoot me?" I asked, my voiced tremoring with fear. I'd like to say that it was put on for effect, but that would be a lie. I had no idea whether my lone escape plan was working or whether I'd survive this horrible experience to live another day. If I did, I'd sure take a lot less for granted going forward.

Like people's guilt or innocence, for one thing.

Diane kicked my leg and lowered the gun from my head to my chest. "That's plan B," she revealed coldly.

"What's plan A?" I whispered as my heart galloped wildly in my chest.

"You like swimming. Don't you, Angie?" she asked, kicking me again. "I figured we could go for a nice night swim at Deadman's Wharf. What do you say?"

"Deadman's Wharf?" I repeated loudly. "But

the undertow there… I wouldn't be able to… I'd…" I cried openly now.

"Oh, I know." Diane's face flashed with sick delight as she loosened the bonds on my ankles. "Now get up."

"I don't want to go to Deadman's Wharf," I wailed. *Please, Octo-Cat. Please be listening. Please understand what I'm trying to tell you.*

"Now it's about what *I* want." She kicked me a third time. "Get up."

Somehow I had to find a way to get up without her seeing my phone on the floor behind me. I made a big show of struggling to my feet then stumbled forward, knocking Diane over in the process.

"Oh, you're going to live to regret that," she growled before breaking out in a creepy laugh. "Luckily it won't be very long."

She pulled us both to our feet, stuck the gun into my ribs, and led me outside. It looked like we were on our way to Deadman's Wharf.

I just hoped we weren't the only ones.

Despite driving in Diane's large luxury SUV,

the ride over was bumpy and painful. Well, I wouldn't be volunteering to lay tied up on the floor again any time soon—that is, if I even managed to reach tomorrow with my life intact.

She'd tied my ankles tight again after forcing me onto the floor of her vehicle, then kept her eyes on me through the rear-view mirror the entire drive over. Even if I'd had the strength to mount an escape, carrying it out would have been impossible under her watchful eye.

By the time we arrived at Deadman's Wharf, I had already lost feeling in my feet. Well, except for the mess of tingles that had taken up residence and made it so that I no longer trusted myself to stand without the very real risk of toppling over.

Diane parked near one of the darkened buildings dotting the wharf and did a quick search of the premises before finally forcing me out of the car.

Wind whipped violently at the waves as Diane dug her nails into my wrist and yanked me toward the nearest pier. But my ankles were still bound too tightly for me to shuffle along. I had to hop along instead, which was especially difficult given the fact my feet had fallen asleep and my brain had gone crazy with fear.

"I did like you before," Diane muttered when we reached the midpoint of the pier. "It's going to be much harder killing you than it was to kill Ethel."

Gee, thanks. She was still going to kill me, but at least she'd feel a little bit bad about it.

"You don't have to do this," I said with great difficulty before falling face forward on the old, weathered planks below when one of my hops failed to land properly.

"Stop being dramatic," Diane hissed in my ear as she put an arm beneath each of mine and pulled me back to a standing position with a series of insulting grunts and groans. "I'd tell you to maybe try a diet, but…" She made a flippant gesture and actually laughed.

"Fat shaming me, really?" I ground out. My legs burned beneath me. The new wounds on my face stung from where my cheek had hit the pier. "I'm sure you'll feel way less guilty about killing me now."

Diane said nothing but quickened our pace toward the end of the pier.

I tried to glance back over my shoulder to see if Octo-Cat and Nan had gotten my message to come out and help. Maybe some lone lobsterman would be out checking his traps. Maybe a car would just randomly happen to pass by…

Or maybe no one was coming.

Maybe I was really going to die.

We were less than ten feet from the end of the pier now. The tide was high and the waves crashed so violently that they lapped at the edge, sending ripples over the wood. I was a good swimmer, having been raised near the ocean, but not nearly good enough to escape waves like this when both my hands and feet were tied tightly.

I had one last chance to make it out of this alive, and it was time for me to take it. Drawing in a deep, labored breath before my next hop, I angled myself so that I landed partially on Diane's foot, knocking us both sideways across the pier.

"Oh, you're going to pay for that!" she whisper-screamed while clutching her jaw from where it had hit on the firm wood planks. I was banking on her to scream and curse at the top of her lungs, but that didn't happen. We didn't both pitch off the side, either.

I glanced around frantically, searching for someone who could save me. *Octo-Cat,* I begged in my mind. *Please, please help me!*

Then I realized I was probably dying one way

or the other, so I began to scream at the top of my lungs, praying with all my might that someone was near, that someone would reach me in time. "Help! She's going to kill me!"

All this did was make Diane even angrier and even more determined to kill me quickly. She hobbled back to her feet. "Thanks for making this so easy, Angie," she growled with animal-like anger in her eyes.

We hadn't reached the end of the pier, but apparently we were close enough. She kicked me in the ribs again and again, forcing me to the edge.

"No, please stop!" I screamed as loud as I could into the empty night.

Much to my surprise, Diane did pause for a moment, regarding me from above with not the slightest flash of pity in her eyes. "You had the chance to stop this, but you just kept digging into things that were none of your business. This isn't my fault. It's yours."

And with that, she swooped down and pushed me with both hands. It was enough to send me rolling straight off the pier and into the unforgiving ocean below.

I sucked in a deep breath just before I hit the

water, just before the darkness of the churning waves pushed me under.

Well, that settled that question. Now I knew…

I was definitely going to die.

CHAPTER NINETEEN

Two near-death experiences within one week has got to be some kind of a record. Then again, time was ticking, and I wasn't sure how much longer I could hold on. No, I probably *wouldn't* survive being pulled down into the undertow of Deadman's Wharf. They called it Deadman's Wharf for a reason, after all.

And if they ever did manage to find my body, it would be far from the first they'd recovered from this perilous stretch of sea.

Diane would be long gone by then.

I thrashed my arms and legs, but only sunk deeper below the waves. The salt of the ocean water stung all my fresh wounds, blinding me with a fresh onslaught of pain. I held my breath past the point of comfort, even as panic overtook me completely. I knew that the first inhalation of sea water would be the thing that ultimately killed me.

But I also knew I didn't want to die.

No matter how much the odds were stacked against me, I had to keep fighting to survive. So, I continued to thrash and hope against hope as the dark depths drew me deeper and deeper into their embrace.

As my brain began to starve from the lack of oxygen, the pain also started to fall away. My body felt lighter, warmer, almost as if it was rising back toward the surface. More likely, though, was that I had died without noticing the exact moment of my demise, and now God was lifting me to Heaven. I even saw a light shining right in my eyes.

And it hurt.

Which meant…

Was I safe now?

I finally gasped for air, unable to hold my breath for even a second longer. The overwhelming pain surged again. It was truly amazing the human capacity for pain. Somehow, I was still finding new ways to hurt, even in the final moments before my death.

I coughed and sputtered, expelling the mistakenly inhaled water in big bursts. A cold chill overtook my entire body when just seconds ago I'd felt warm and peaceful. Even though it felt as if they were weighted down by heavy blocks, I managed to open my eyes just long enough to notice I wasn't underwater anymore.

Somebody pulled me up and onto the pier, and somebody else climbed up after. Had he been the one to pull me to the surface?

I didn't have time to figure out their identities, because everything went dark again as I lost consciousness.

Yes, *again.*

Yes, that makes three times so far this week.

This was by far the worst, though.

My throat was on fire as I vomited lava onto the ground beside me. At least that's what it felt like.

Nan's voice was the first I discerned from the jumble surrounding me. "That's right, dear. Cough it all out."

I took her advice and coughed and coughed

until it didn't hurt quite so bad. When I opened my eyes to see who had saved me, I came face to face with a set of amber eyes glinting in the darkness as they regarded me with pity.

No, not pity. *Fear.*

Octo-Cat's entire body shook, and I didn't think it was from the dampness of his fur or the chilliness of the night. "I thought I'd lost you now, too," he said between panicked kitty breaths.

"I'm okay," I said, reaching out to pet him. My hand came away soaked, making me wonder if he'd jumped in after me despite his hatred of any water that didn't come from an Evian bottle.

I continued to stroke him until his labored breathing became gentler and was ultimately drowned out by the beautiful, contented sound of his rumbling purr.

"Diane Fulton," I ground out, sputtering even still. "Did she get away?"

A familiar pair of strong arms lifted me to a sitting position and wrapped a shiny insulated blanket over my shoulders. "We got her," the police officer said with a reassuring smile. Seeing as he was just as drenched as I was, I assumed this was the brave man who had jumped in to save me before Deadman's Wharf could claim me forever.

Nan appeared at my side, sitting right down on the pier and crossing her legs like we were at a slumber party and not a rescue mission. "That was good thinking, calling your iPad," she told me, careful to leave out any direct references to Octo-Cat I noticed. "We were able to record our end of the line and gave it to the police as evidence. And her intention to kill you," Nan revealed, rubbing my shoulder over the insulated blanket. "It was just awful to listen to, especially when the call went silent."

My heart clenched, reimagining tonight's events from poor Nan's perspective. Luckily, she was a tough, old kook, and I seemed to be okay now.

"Of course, you're going to need to buy me a new iPad now," Octo-Cat added, pushing his way under the blanket with me. "And seeing all you put me through tonight, you might have to make that two iPads."

"You did the right thing," the officer told Nan. "Your quick thinking saved your daughter's life."

"Oh, granddaughter, actually." Nan giggled and coquettishly twirled a ringlet as she looked the officer up and down. The officer, who was way, way too young for her to be flirting with. "What's your name again?"

Some things never changed, and thank goodness for that.

"Officer Damon Bouchard, ma'am." He smiled kindly at her, but I felt Nan stiffen beside me at the polite nickname. Her crush had ended just as soon as it had begun. That was good considering we had enough to deal with already.

"Are you ready to get in the ambulance?" the other officer asked—a woman—approaching us from the pier.

"Can my cat come, too?"

Officer Bouchard shrugged and glanced toward his partner. "I guess he can ride over with us, but unfortunately he's not going to be able to come into the hospital with us."

"But…" I hesitated. After all we'd just been through, I didn't want to leave him again especially so soon.

"It's okay, dear," Nan said, turning her full focus to me once again. "I'll take care of him until you're well enough to come home."

"Could you just give me a moment alone with him?" I asked, knowing the request made me sound crazy.

"Um, sure," Officer Bouchard said.

"We'll just be over there," the other officer said, pointing somewhere to the right, but I didn't care enough to notice.

"You can stay, Nan," I said as she began to struggle to her feet.

She settled back down and wrapped both arms around me, then we waited together until we knew we had the privacy we needed.

"Thank you for saving my life," I whispered toward my chest, where Octo-Cat still sat nuzzled against me. "I'm sorry I scruffed you, and I'm sorry for all the times I was rude or didn't understand. During this past week you've become my best friend... well, other than Nan, I mean... and I'm so glad you're in my life. Can you forgive me?"

A few tense moments of silence passed before Octo-Cat finally extracted himself from the warmth of the blanket and came to stand before me on the wharf. "You're my best friend, too," he said, rubbing his head against my hand and purring in earnest. "But if you ever scruff me again, I'll kill you and eat the evidence."

I erupted with laughter, and Nan joined me even though she didn't quite know why.

"Thank you for avenging Ethel," he said when

our peals of laughter faded out. "She would have liked you, you know."

My eyes teared at the compliment. *Ugh,* more salt water was not what I needed just then. Still, judging from how awesome her cat was, I bet I would have liked her, too.

CHAPTER TWENTY

I felt fine—all things considering—but the hospital insisted on keeping me for at least twenty-four hours since I was still in danger of succumbing to my near-drowning even now.

I groaned audibly when a familiar face popped into my room.

"So..." Dr. Artie Lewis, the same ER doctor who had treated me earlier that week, said with an obnoxiously large smile. "You decided to up the ante this time, eh? You know, real life isn't an action movie. You can't keep putting your life at risk and expecting to survive."

Yes, this was the same guy who had made me feel like an idiot when I came to him for care after getting zapped unconscious by the office coffeemaker. It was upsetting to see that his bedside manner hadn't improved since I'd seen him last.

The doctor bobbed his head, ignoring the fact that I hadn't responded to his greeting—or his advice. "Drowning is definitely a more impressive way to lose consciousness. Good job."

Did he really just compliment me on my method of getting hurt? Yeah, because I had a lot of control over that. I briefly wondered if perhaps the not-so-good doc was a bit of a thrill seeker in his life outside of the hospital. He seemed almost excited as he discussed the details of my near drowning.

"Just leave me alone," I pleaded, finally breaking my silence. Hadn't I already been through enough that day?

I'd nearly died, for crying out loud!

He shot me a withering glance before chuckling to himself and saying, "No can do. This time you need a lot more than some regular strength Tylenol. You know, a smile wouldn't hurt you much, either."

If I had any strength left, I'd have shot out of bed to punch him in the face. I'd had enough violence for one day, however—even though it sure seemed like this doctor guy was cut from the same sleazy cloth as my least favorite colleague, Brad.

Maybe it was time to start exploring some alternative medicine therapies... or to stop getting knocked unconscious every other day. Either worked.

"I'll be back later," Dr. Lewis announced after a brief glance over my vitals. "By the way, you have some guests waiting in the lobby. Should I send them in?"

"Yes, please." I nodded excitedly, wondering if Nan had somehow found a way to sneak Octo-Cat into my room. I definitely wouldn't put it past her.

It wasn't Nan who came to see me, though.

A few minutes later, Mr. Fulton and Bethany shuffled into my room. Mr. Fulton carried a giant pink teddy bear that said *It's a Girl* which made me giggle.

Ouch. Laughing hurt deep in my chest.

"How are you doing?" Bethany asked, trailing her fingers along the foot of my bed. I'd never seen her out of office clothes before and was surprised to find her personal style was actually pretty fun. She wore red polka dotted pants with a white button down shirt, an outfit that would have fit perfectly with either Nan's or my own wardrobe.

"Pretty good, considering." I smiled to show her

I was all right and that there were no hard feelings between us.

"I'm sorry my wife almost killed you," Mr. Fulton interjected, catching me off guard. I mean, I'd only been in the hospital a few hours. It seemed strange that he and Bethany already knew what had happened.

"How did you find out?" I asked, wondering just how much he knew about what had transpired between me and Diane, if he knew that she was also to blame for killing his beloved aunt.

He rushed to explain. "I came home from my trip early and saw your car in front of my house and the door wide open. A short while later, officers showed up and brought me in for questioning. Let's just say they caught me up on my wife's shocking extracurricular activities."

"And you?" I asked Bethany. I remembered now that, in the middle of her maniacal raving, Diane had mentioned something about Bethany being Mr. Fulton's daughter. I still had so many questions about that but was hoping they might fill me in without being prompted. After all, it technically wasn't any of my business.

Bethany glanced toward Mr. Fulton nervously. "He called me on the way over."

"It's okay," I coaxed, apparently unable to play it cool. "Diane told me the truth. At least, I think she did."

I turned to Mr. Fulton. "Is she really your daughter?"

"Yes," they answered in unison, both regarding me with similar expressions.

"How come you didn't just tell me that?" I asked Bethany, recalling the hard time I'd given her at the funeral. Of course, I felt terrible now.

"I didn't want it getting out," Mr. Fulton explained. "Diane was already so upset."

I glanced back toward Bethany. "Did you know all this time?"

"Not all this time. I suspected he might be my mysterious missing father when I took my position at the firm, but we only just had it verified by DNA testing. In fact, that's why I decided to apply in the first place."

Mr. Fulton looked like he was going to be sick as he explained, "I cheated on Diane while we were dating. Just once, but—"

"It led to my mom getting pregnant," Bethany supplied. "I've had some strange... health issues these past few years, and I've been trying to learn more about my best options. So, finally my mom caved and told me more about my father."

"Oh," I said simply. It sucked for Diane that her husband had cheated on her. Sure, they hadn't been married at that time, but they'd still been committed to each other. You always assume that your partner will be faithful—but then again, you also assume they won't try to murder anyone you care about, too.

"We figured since you were already part of the family drama, thanks to Diane, you at least deserved to know the full story," she said with a sniff.

"I'm so sorry, Bethany. I treated you horribly." It all came rushing to me then. She'd grown up without a dad. She'd suffered health issues she didn't feel comfortable disclosing, and she'd recently lost an aunt she never even got the chance to know.

"Yes, you did," Bethany said with a frown that quickly transformed into a smile. "But I've treated you horribly on so many other occasions that perhaps we're just even now. Let's stop trying to tear each other down and start lifting each other up instead now, okay?"

"We girls have to stick together," I said in agreement. "By the way, I really like your outfit."

She smiled and sashayed playfully at the compliment.

"Again, I'm so sorry that my wife tried to kill you," Mr. Fulton said with a pained expression. "What I don't understand is why. Do you know?"

Both he and Bethany studied me with curious eyes.

I took a deep breath to steady myself before revealing, "She thought I was psychic and that I had figured everything out. As part of that, she confessed to killing Ethel in a scheme to get more money out of your divorce."

Mr. Fulton sighed and shook his head.

"Are you?" Bethany asked, her breathing hitched slightly as she awaited my response.

I scrunched up my face in confusion. "Am I what?"

"Psychic," she supplied.

"What?" I chuckled nervously. No one besides Nan could ever know the truth about me and Octo-Cat. "No, of course not. Don't be silly."

Bethany laughed, too. "Just seeing if you still have your wits about you after that massive loss of oxygen to your brain."

Mr. Fulton placed a hand on his daughter's shoulder. "Bethany, could you give us a moment?"

"Sure. I'll be waiting for you outside," she answered, smiling at me one more time before leaving the room and clicking the door shut behind her.

Fulton grabbed a nearby chair and pulled it up beside my bed. "I think it goes without saying I'll be resigning from the firm."

I nodded, unsure of what he wanted from me now.

"I'll actually be using it as an opportunity to retire, get to know my daughter, and enjoy life outside of work for a change."

"That's great," I said, happy for him but finding it hard to maintain my enthusiasm. My brain felt heavy with the weight of all the new knowledge I'd acquired that day, and I needed my rest.

"I had no idea what Diane was up to all this time, but I'm so sorry you got hurt because of it." He reached into his suit jacket and pulled out a check book. "I know I can never make it fully right, but let me help you somehow. Do you think one hundred thousand is enough to…? Well, to forgive me?"

I edged my hand toward his, but couldn't quite reach. "You don't need to pay me off. I forgive you."

"Please let me do something. This money and more was going to go to Diane in the divorce, but now that she'll probably be spending the rest of her life in prison, I suddenly have far more than I need." He seemed so sad, so desperate to give me a small fortune in recompense. But he had never done anything wrong. Well, not for the past thirtyish years, at least.

"I don't need anything," I said, realizing as soon as I said the words that they weren't entirely true.

Mr. Fulton must have caught onto my ambivalence, because he said, "I can see you do. How about one hundred and fifty? Two hundred? Please, just tell me what you need."

For the briefest of moments, I allowed myself to envision what life would be like with that kind of money. I could stop working, put a sizable down payment on a house all my own, or even take a couple years off to travel the world.

I could do anything my little heart desired.

But, honestly, I liked my life, no matter how lackluster it may appear to an outsider. Sure, I wanted to be rich one day—*who doesn't?*—but I also wanted to make my own fortune, my own way.

There was one thing, however, I now desperately wanted that only Mr. Fulton could provide.

"I do have a request, if you don't mind," I said after licking my cracked and dried lips.

He perked right up and poised his pen over the checkbook. "Anything. Name your price."

"Would you mind if I keep the cat?" I asked, almost afraid to breathe until he gave me his answer.

He closed his checkbook and stared at me blankly. "The cat?" he asked to clarify.

"Yeah, Octavius Maxwell..." I broke off in a laugh. "You know, Ethel's cat, the one I've been looking after this week."

"The cat!" Recognition at last lighted in his eyes. "I forgot about him with everything else that's been going on these past few days."

I smiled and waited for his answer.

It came with a wink that I didn't quite understand. "Of course, you can have the cat. I'll send over his things in a couple days when you're settled back at home."

My heart filled with joy over being able to keep an animal I had until very recently considered the bane of my existence, but now wouldn't trade for the world—or for two-hundred thousand dollars.

"Thank you so much," I called after Mr.

Fulton's departing figure, absolutely beside myself with delight.

I couldn't wait to get home and tell Octo-Cat the good news.

I was given the next two weeks off work to recover from my ordeal and spent most of it curled up on the couch with Octo-Cat, catching up on all our favorite human TV shows. We even found a show about a cat trainer, which we both found hilarious. Every time the "expert" interpreted what the cat was feeling, Octo-Cat corrected him and we both broke out laughing.

A few days into my forced vacation time—yeah, they really had to twist my arm on this one—a parcel arrived by courier.

"What's this?" I asked, after signing my name on the dotted line.

He shrugged and trotted away, leaving me alone with the mysterious letter. It was a very thick letter, at least twenty pages long.

"Whatcha got there?" Octo-Cat asked, coming to sit beside me at the table as I continued to puzzle over the manila envelope lying before me.

"I honestly have no idea," I answered while fiddling with the clasp.

"Well, open up! I'm dying of curiosity here."

I decided to let that one go, since I was also quite curious myself.

After pulling out the bundle of pages, I quickly scanned the first, then flipped through, glazing over the headlines for each subsequent section of the legal document before me.

"Say, Octo-Cat," I murmured, unable to tear my eyes away. "What's your full name again?"

"Octavius Maxwell Ricardo Edmund Frederick Fulton Russo," he said, each syllable rolling off his sandpaper tongue seamlessly.

"Aww," I cooed. "You added my last name."

"Well, of course, I did. You're my human," he said with an endearing twitch of his whiskers.

"Um, for legal purposes, you'll have to drop the Russo, though."

"Why?"

I pushed the papers toward him, even though he couldn't read very well yet.

"What's that say?" His tail flicked in agitation.

"This is the paperwork for the trust fund Ethel set up for you. Now that you live with me, I'm your official guardian and thus guarantor of your estate."

He yawned. "And that means?"

"Two things," I told him with a huge smile on my face. "One, you're legally mine now. And two, we will receive a stipend of five thousand dollars per month to contribute to your care and provide the lifestyle to which you are accustomed."

Octo-Cat's eyes grew wide.

"Finally!" he cried. "I knew Ethel would come through for me. Now let's have a little talk about these living quarters…"

WHAT'S NEXT?

I'm finally coming to terms with the fact I can speak to animals, even though the only one who ever talks back is the crabby tabby I've taken to calling Octo-Cat. What I haven't quite worked out is how to hide my secret...

Now one of the associates at my law firm has discovered this strange new talent of mine and insists I use it to help defend his client against a double murder charge. To make things worse, Octo-Cat has no intention of helping either of us.

Our only hope rests on a spastic Yorkie named Yo-Yo, who hasn't quite figured out his owner is dead. Can we find a way to get Yo-Yo to help solve the murder without breaking his poor doggie heart?

SNEAK PEEK OF TERRIER TRANSGRESSIONS

Hi, I'm Angie Russo, and I have a talking cat for a pet. Well, he only talks to me, but still. A few months have passed since he came to live with me following the murder of his owner—a sweet old lady who was poisoned by a member of her own family in a greedy inheritance grab.

Since then, Octo-Cat and I have been settling into our new life as roommates, and he's nice to me more often than not just so long as I feed him his breakfast on time and never, ever call him "kitty." He's even learned how to use his iPad to call me on FaceTime so we can check in with each other while I'm at work.

Yes, *his* iPad.

Have I mentioned just how spoiled he is?

Not only does he have his own tablet—and a trust fund, too—but he insists on drinking Evian fresh from the bottle and will only eat certain flavors of Fancy Feast when served on specific dishes and according to his rigorously kept, though fully unnecessary, schedule.

I have to admit he's grown on me, something I honestly never thought would happen. I even kind of like my job as a paralegal at Fulton, Thompson and Associates these days. Things have been pretty interesting since the Fultons left town rather abruptly and our firm lost its senior most partner.

A cutthroat competition as to who will take his place has ensued. Until Mr. Thompson decides whom he'd like to promote, though, we're simply Thompson and Associates. Lots of candidates—both from within our firm and from outside—have been passing through our office in hopes of securing the coveted position at Blueberry Bay's most respected law firm, but Thompson is having a hard time making up his mind.

Can't say I blame him. I definitely wouldn't want to be in his shoes.

Our firm is now a bit infamous following the surprising murder involving one of its partners and his family. Everyone wants the scoop, but Mr.

Thompson has made it very clear: we aren't supposed to discuss what happened with anyone.

In the meantime, he has hired a new associate to help keep up with the newly increased workload. Charles Longfellow, III, came to us highly recommended with a great resume and even better looks.

It's been a while since I've had a crush but—boy—do I have it bad for Charlie. He's got this thick, wavy hair that falls in a perfect dark swoop on his forehead. He's tall, like *maybe played basketball in high school but probably not in college* tall, and you could easily get lost in his deep green eyes. I know, because I already have a few times.

Yes, as much as I usually prefer books to boys, I often find myself a bit twitterpated whenever Charles is near. That's probably how I made such a colossal mistake in the first place…

Now I'm being blackmailed about my biggest secret, the fact that I can talk to animals.

The worst part? I kind of like it.

I should probably start at the beginning, huh?

Well, here goes nothing…

Octo-Cat called me via FaceTime just before noon.

I was at the office, of course, but since he knew not to call unless it was an emergency, I decided to put my research on hold to answer him. Besides, almost everyone had left the firm for an early lunch meeting, leaving me more or less alone in the building.

"What do you need?" I asked after scanning the premises just in case I wasn't as alone as I'd thought. Normally I took my calls with Octo-Cat in the bathroom, but one of the junior associates had been holed up in there for at least half an hour before he left—and I definitely wanted to avoid whatever disaster scenario he'd left behind.

"There's a fly in my Evian," my cat complained with a keening mewl. His face looked utterly scandalized as he leaned in close to the camera.

"Oh, you poor thing," I cooed while rolling my eyes just out of his view. Octo-Cat was definitely too spoiled for his own good sometimes, but then again, I received a five-thousand-dollar monthly allowance for his care, so I really couldn't complain too much.

"My thoughts exactly," he answered with a grimace and a sigh. "I need you to come home immediately to rectify this situation."

"I can't. I'm at work," I reminded him with a beleaguered sigh of my own while clicking through my overfull email inbox idly.

Octo-Cat growled when he noticed he didn't have my full attention. "I thought you were supposed to only be going part-time now?"

Why was I constantly explaining my life choices to a cat? He rarely remembered what I told him, anyway. We'd had this exact same conversation about my work at least three times already. Rehashing it now felt like the ultimate exercise in futility.

Still, it was easier to explain yet again than to deal with one of his hissy fits.

"Yes, technically I am part-time," I explained patiently. "But I need to help out extra until Thompson finally hires a new partner. It's been really busy around here, and unfortunately, I just don't have time to stop home and pour you a new cup of water right now. I'm sorry."

His eyes narrowed, ready to go to war over such a simple thing. "But don't you receive a generous monthly stipend to ensure I'm cared for in the manner to which I am accustomed? Because I most definitely am *not* accustomed to having a wiggly-legged fly swimming in my Evian."

Once again, it was easier to cave than it was to argue for hours or days on end. "*Aargh*, fine. I'll send Nan by to pour you some more water. Happy?"

He yawned, which only annoyed me more. "Not exactly. It will take me days to recover from this horrible event. Could you make sure Nan knows she needs to throw out the contaminated cup?"

"You are a cat," I said between clenched teeth. "You are supposed to be a fearsome hunter, not a spoiled baby. You know, other cats even—"

"Angie?" a deep, dreamy voice broke into the middle of our conversation.

Oh, no, no, no. Everyone was supposed to be gone!

I spun around in my chair to find none other than Charles Longfellow, III standing behind me and gawking over my shoulder at the image of Octo-Cat on my phone screen.

"Um, hi, Charles." I tittered nervously as I pushed the button to end our call, but it was too late. He'd already heard and seen more than enough to figure out my secret. The best I could hope for now is that he would think one or both of us had gone crazy.

I took it as a good sign that he stood looking at me as if I'd sprouted a second head. Perhaps that would have been less strange than what he'd really walked in on.

"Is everything all right?" he asked, raising one thick eyebrow in my direction. The air suddenly felt impossibly thin like the office had been transported to the top of the nearest mountain.

I nodded, desperate for Charles to go away and stop questioning me. "Perfectly all right. Thanks," I lied, wishing I'd inherited Nan's legendary acting skills. As it was, I could tell my colleague wasn't fooled by my feeble attempts to downplay the situation.

Sure enough, his voice dripped with sarcasm as he said, "Really? Because it seemed like your cat needed some help with his..." A delicious smile crept across his face, stretching from one high cheek bone to the next. "Evian? Is that right?"

My mouth fell open from shock, but no additional words came out to explain away the freak show my crush had just witnessed.

"Well?" he prompted, widening his eyes at me. "Were you or were you not just having a conversation with your cat?"

I tucked my hair behind my ears and swallowed hard before stumbling over my answer. "Um, I call him sometimes when I'm away. He has separation anxiety so..." I gave him my most ingratiating smile, but it didn't seem to work. I was seriously outmatched here.

"But it sounded like maybe he was talking back to you," Charles insisted. "Like you were having an actual conversation with each other."

I blinked hard as I stammered, "What? No, don't be silly. Of course, I can't talk to animals. I mean, who can?"

"You, apparently," Charles said, narrowing his gaze at me. Clearly, he wasn't going to let me off the hook until I revealed the one thing I most wanted to hide.

I swallowed the giant lump that had become lodged in my throat, then broke out in hysterical laughter. *"Gotcha!* I can't believe you fell for my little office prank."

Charles shoved both hands in his pockets and rocked back and forth on his heels, but didn't say anything.

Oh my gosh. Why wasn't he saying anything?

My heart galloped like a wild stallion as my nervous laughter fell away.

Charles studied me for a long time, and stupidly I couldn't bring myself to look away. "You're coming with me," he said.

"What?" I crossed my arms over my chest in

defiance. "No. I have too much work to catch up on here."

He placed his palms on my desk and leaned down so our faces were only a few inches apart. Given pretty much any other circumstance, I'd have enjoyed having his gorgeous face so near to mine.

As it was now, though? I was absolutely terrified.

"You're coming with me," he repeated with a devilish grin. "Unless you want me to tell everyone what I saw."

I gulped. "Everyone?"

"Everyone," he confirmed before returning to his full height and straightening his tie.

Completely bewildered and unable to see any practical alternative, I rose to join Charles.

"Excellent," he said, leading me to the door and motioning for me to go through it.

I turned back to study him. "Where are we going?"

"My place," he answered coolly as we strode through the parking lot toward his car. Charles had never invited me anywhere before, especially not his apartment. Unfortunately, something told me I wouldn't like what was waiting for me there one bit.

ABOUT MOLLY FITZ

Molly Fitz is the quirky, cozy mystery pen name of USA Today bestselling author Melissa Storm. And while she can't technically talk to animals, she and her doggie best friend, Sky Princess, have deep and very animated conversations as they navigate their days. Add to that five more dogs, a snarky feline, comedian husband, and diva daughter, and you can pretty much imagine how life looks in the Casa de Fitz.

Molly lives in a house on a high hill in the Michigan woods and occasionally ventures out for good food, great coffee, or to meet new animal friends. Head to

www.MollyMysteries.com for more Molly, or www.
MelStorm.com to learn about her alter ego, Melissa.

MORE FROM MOLLY

If you're ready to dive right in to more Pet Whisperer
P.I., then you can even keep an eye out for the next
books in the series:

Terrier Transgressions
Hairless Harassment
Dog-Eared Delinquent

CONNECT WITH MOLLY

Sign up for Molly's newsletter for book updates and cat
pics: **mollymysteries.com/subscribe**

Download Molly's app for cool bonus content:
mollymysteries.com/app

Join Molly's reader group on Facebook to make new
friends: **mollymysteries.com/group**

Made in the USA
Coppell, TX
05 September 2020

35725763R10142